D1714365

A Violent Outcome
A Rab Sinclair Western

◇

Robert Peecher

For information the author may be contacted at

PO Box 967; Watkinsville GA; 30677

or at mooncalfpress.com

FOR JEAN

- 1 -

The blue roan with the black face struck a fine impression with its easy gait.

The rider sat tall in the saddle, broad shouldered and confident as he rode. But he held his reins easy and gave every appearance of being relaxed as the roan trotted past the old Catholic mission and into the Las Vegas square.

Past a certain hour of the early evening, decent folks stayed out of the square, and it was getting nigh on that time.

The big hotel on the corner and its restaurant still attracted an acceptable clientele, and the shops on the square did a trade with family folks and ranchers. But the men who frequented the saloons off the square almost all bore names that appeared on warrants in one place or another. Much past sundown, good folks had to be willing to tolerate a certain amount of harassment if they walked the streets.

Petty thefts were also becoming a problem.

The rider passed through the square and drew reins out front of a saloon just a block north of the plaza.

Over the saddle horn the rider had a saddle holster with a big Colt Dragoon. He'd recently taken it to a gunsmith there in Las Vegas and had the gun converted to accept metal cartridges.

He sat his saddle for a moment, thinking about whether or not to tuck the Dragoon into his belt. He'd not come looking for trouble.

He took his pipe from the pocket of his buckskin coat and filled it, striking a match against the rough, coiled rope beside his leg. He puffed the pipe a few times to get the tobacco in the bowl to light.

In the end, it wasn't the trouble in the saloon that made him decide to tote the gun, but the thieves without it.

If it was not for the propensity for the roan to take a bite out of strangers, he'd have worried whether or not the horse would be there when he came out. But it would take a wily man to steal this horse.

"All right, you old biter," the man said, dropping down out of the saddle and giving the blue roan a rub on the neck. "I ain't gonna be but a minute. You hang tight out here and don't let nobody ride off with you."

The saloon did not have a signboard posted out front, but it wouldn't have mattered if it did. The rider never learned to read letters.

Alternately, the place was known as the Robins Nest and Hank Little's Place.

The Robins Nest was a play on words, of sorts.

Among the local population of thieves and ne'er-do-wells, they had started calling it "The Robbers Roost." But then they decided they wanted to be a bit more subtle, so they called it the Robins Nest.

Hank Little was the owner of the establishment. Hank was a good sort and had been in Las Vegas for some years now, but he was getting older and less discerning in his clientele, and anymore if a saloonkeeper wanted to stay in business, he had to accept all kinds.

The rider dropped the big Colt Dragoon into the holster on his thigh. He wore it low, finding it easier to reach for if it was lower down on his leg. Most times, he'd slide the leather thong over the hammer to help hold the gun in place, but if he thought he might need in the gun in a hurry he left the thong off. Just in case, he now left the thong hanging.

In the light of dusk, the rider stepped into the saloon.

Hank Little's Place was pretty dark just now. A couple of oil lanterns burned on a cabinet behind the bar, and there were four lit lanterns hanging on chains from the ceiling. But there were lots of places inside the saloon where the light did not easily reach.

To his right was the bar, with Hank Little behind it and four men sitting on stools along the length of the bar. They were sitting with space between them, suggesting all four of them were alone.

To his left, there were tables along the wall. Only two of the tables were occupied. Two men sat at a table near the front of the saloon, but in the back, left corner there were six men gathered around a table.

In the center of the saloon there were four faro

tables, but only one dealer sat at a table and three players sat in front of him.

"Rabbie Sinclair?" Hank Little said. "I haven't seen you in months."

"Evening, Hank," Rab Sinclair said, removing the pipe from his mouth. Deliberately, he used his left hand to remove the pipe and hold it so that his right hand would be free.

"What can I do you for?"

"Nothing tonight, Hank," Sinclair said. Nodding at the back table, he added, "I've come for this one."

Hank looked at the table. A bunch of young faces. If they were of a certain age and he hadn't seen them in months, Hank Little still didn't forget them. But if they were younger, even if they came in his saloon every night of the week and twice on Saturdays, he couldn't remember their names.

The folks at the table in the back were all too young for Hank to know, though he'd seen their faces a number of times in the last few days.

A dark-complexioned man with jet black hair at the back table stood up. He wore a brown coat that was patched in odd places and loose-fitting trousers. It was a job the trousers had to be loose, because Chavez was a heavily built man, and clothes of any sort had to work at being loose on him.

He did not wear a gunbelt because of the way his belly folded over, but on the table in front of him there was a short-barreled scatter gun.

"You've come for which one?" he asked. "You've come for me?"

"Sit down, Chavez," Rab Sinclair said. "Don't be begging for trouble where none exists. I've come for Caleb Morgan. Come on now, son."

The man named Chavez did not sit down, and the boy named Caleb Morgan did not get up.

"I don't remember you, that's telling him what to do, being his pa," Chavez said.

Chavez was a local troublemaker. His mother's people were Mexican and had lived here almost as long as the Spanish mission had been here. Like so many others in the area, when the treaty of Guadalupe-Hidalgo was signed and the New Mexico Territory was formed, his mother's people stayed and became Americans.

Chavez's mother fell in love with a white trapper who was working in the Pecos River valley beyond Hermit Creek. They married, and she fell pregnant. Before the boy was born, the trapper went back over Hermit Peak and never came back. Some years later they found his body in a ravine where he'd fallen. Chavez came up a split personality, living part way in two different worlds, neither of which completely accepted him. He was big and dumb and not near as tough as he liked to think he was.

Sinclair had hired him once to do some work on his ranch east of town, but Chavez never had a man to teach him how to work, and he'd only lasted a couple of days before Sinclair sent him off for loafing.

Sinclair saw a trail of smoke drifting up from his pipe, and he raised it up and took a draw on it, blowing out the smoke and giving time for Chavez's challenge to hang in the air for a moment.

"And I don't remember you, that's talking to me, having the gumption to face a man," Sinclair said. He said it with an amused grin and in such a calm and light tone that no one took Rab's words as a threat. Even the boys sitting at the table with Chavez had to crack smiles. "So sit down, Chavez, before you get into something you don't have the gumption to be in."

Rab Sinclair had an easy way about him. He took a taunt without getting riled, and that sometimes made a certain sort get angrier still. Chavez was that sort, and he was fuming.

"I'll show you gumption," Chavez said, and he stepped away from the table and out into the aisle between tables against the wall and the faro tables.

Everyone in the saloon was watching now.

Chavez took a tentative step to see what Rab Sinclair would do, and when he simply drew on his pipe, Chavez decided to make a charge.

He was like a bull at the stampede coming forward.

With the toe of his boot, Rab Sinclair slid a chair away from the nearest table and then kicked it so that it slid forward into Chavez's path. The big man ran into the chair and fell headlong. Rab stepped aside, giving him room to land, and then he pulled the heavy Colt Dragoon from its holster.

In one fast motion, Sinclair dropped to a knee and swung the Dragoon down from over his head. The barrel of the gun cracked Chavez in the back of the head, stunning the hell out of him.

Then Sinclair was standing again, his thumb on the hammer of the gun and the barrel pointed generally at the back table.

"Caleb Morgan," Rab Sinclair said, and the light, easy

tone was gone from his voice. "Get up from that table and come with me."

Caleb was round about twenty years old now. His ma and pa were both dead, and the old man who cared for him for a number of years was dead, too. A couple of years back, Rab took him in. He built a little cabin for Caleb on his place and hired him to help work the ranch.

But lately Caleb had taken to making bad decisions and running with a bad crowd. His work on the ranch wasn't getting done the way it should.

None of them at the back table were very old. They were all around Caleb's age. But the oldest among them, a man who Rab Sinclair did not recognize, spoke up.

"Best go on, Caleb," he said. "Nobody here is looking for any trouble."

Caleb didn't say a word. He just stood up and started walking toward the door.

Rab dropped the Dragoon back in his holster and took a couple of steps backwards toward the door, keeping his eyes on the back table. He pushed the door open and held it for Caleb as he walked by.

"I'll be seeing you, Hank," Sinclair said to the barman.

Outside, Caleb stepped into the saddle on the big bay he was riding, and Rab Sinclair got back onto the blue roan.

"You don't have to come to town to fetch me," Caleb pouted. "I can make my own decisions."

"Don't you act like a child with me," Rab Sinclair said. "I ain't your pa, and I ain't going to tolerate peevish behavior. But you told Evangeline that you'd be around for supper this evening. When you weren't there, she was worried and sent me to find you. I ain't yet et, and I'm feeling a mite indisposed toward you right now."

As the horses started out of town, Caleb Morgan dropped his head.

"I'm sorry Rab," he said. "I plumb forgot about supper."

"Save your apologies for the woman who cooked for you."

***

The night was pitch black by the time the two riders neared Sinclair's ranch. But the darkness did not bother either the riders or the horses. They could all find their way in the dark. The path to the ranch was pretty well worn, and the horses could be trusted.

The ranch sat down in a valley framed by long mesas dotted with juniper. The mesas confined the cattle and made life difficult for rustlers. Sinclair's cabin was nestled below a tall, rocky cliff, the top of which was crowded with ponderosa pines. At times, Rab Sinclair liked to go and sit on a rocky ledge and just look out through the valley.

From the ledge, he could see Starvation Peak to the southeast.

Starvation Peak, with its easily recognizable curving slopes and flat top, was like a touchstone that gave Sinclair a sense of home. Whenever he was close enough to see it, he knew he was no more than a day's ride from being back at his place.

But sometimes, too, the tall peak could feel like an

anchor, weighing him down and keeping him locked to where he was.

His mood dictated the way he felt about the peak, and his mood could be a shifting thing, even when the peak was solid and unchanging.

They'd ridden in silence most of the way back from the Las Vegas plaza. Caleb Morgan wrestled against an inner turmoil that Rab Sinclair could not understand.

Like Caleb, Rab Sinclair lost everyone when he was young. His mother died before he ever knew who she was. Raised by his father, a Scotch preacher who traveled among the People as a missionary, passed on when Rab was a teenager.

But at that point, Sinclair was alone and having to make do for himself. He had no one to watch out for him or raise him, and he went overnight from being someone's son to being a man making his own way.

Caleb was different in that he always had someone watching out for him, and somewhere along the line Caleb had failed to make the transition into manhood.

They rode their horses down to the barn. Rab lit a lantern and they unsaddled the horses and brushed them down before turning them out.

"Wash up and come in for your supper," Sinclair said. "If it's still warm, that'll be a miracle."

Rab Sinclair went first to the wash basin on the side of the cabin and washed his face and hands. The towel was fresh, so he actually came out of it cleaner than he'd been going into the washing.

"The prodigal has returned," Rab said, walking into the cabin while Caleb was still washing up.

Evangeline was standing at the stove.

"I heard you ride up and saw the light down at the barn," she said. "I put the food back on the stove to warm it up."

"You're a better woman than I deserve," Rab said.

He'd found Evangeline some years before in a saloon in Santa Fe. She'd come up in California, the daughter of a gold prospector who never found enough gold to keep his family fed. Her mother turned cook for their camp, and men in California in those days paid a premium for food cooked by a woman's hand. So Evangeline grew up helping her mother and became herself a better cook than most.

"Where'd you find him?" she asked.

Rab took a seat at the table, looking at the shape of the woman at the stove. Evangeline was long-legged and lean, but stronger than a person might think. She took to work easy, and her hands were often as blistered as Rab's. She also took easy to a saddle, and she could ride like a Comanche.

"You're as good a hand as a man could want, you know that?" Rab said, exposing his thoughts.

Evangeline laughed.

"That's not what I asked. I asked where you found Caleb."

As she repeated the question, though, the door to the cabin opened and Caleb Morgan walked in, still drying his hands on his trousers.

"Sorry, Miss Evangeline," Caleb said. "I told you this morning that I'd be here for supper, and I just forgot."

Rab Sinclair nodded to the younger man to

acknowledge the decent manners.

His Scotch father, a Presbyterian, raised young Rabbie among the Indians, traveling from one settlement or camp to the next.

The Sioux and Cheyenne, the Cherokee and the Osage, the Arapaho and the Ute. There were others, too. He was never around long enough to learn much of their languages – a little here and there, but he learned a great deal of their customs.

Through it all, the old Scotsman endeavored to learn his son decent manners.

Caleb took a seat at the table, and Evangeline carried plates from the stove to the table for both men, and then she went back to fetch one for herself.

"There in Hank Little's place, who was the older feller settin' with you?" Rab asked Caleb, as much to learn the answer as to answer Evangeline's question.

"None of 'em was older," Caleb said.

"One looked to be older than the others," Rab said.

Only in his mid-thirties, Rab didn't yet have enough years behind him to have a son of Caleb's age, but the difference in maturity made them very much like father and son sometimes.

Rab had purposefully tried to stray from such a relationship. Caleb only lived in Rab's cabin temporarily while they built the boy a cabin of his own. Rab paid Caleb wages, and Caleb in turn paid back a small rent to Sinclair. And, unless Caleb promised to be at supper and didn't show up, Rab Sinclair let the boy come and go as he wanted, so long as the work was done.

"You're probably talking about Matty Rio," Caleb

said.

"Kind of a fancy dresser," Rab said.

He'd noticed that right away about the man who told Caleb to go on – the man Caleb obeyed.

He wore a white shirt adorned with black stitching and a black vest with similar stitching in white. His hatband bore two rows of silver studs.

"He's got nice clothes," Caleb said. "There's nothing wrong with nice clothes."

"I reckon not," Rab said, slipping a glance to Evangeline.

She frowned at Rab.

"We're taking some beeves up to the fort in the morning," Evangeline said. "You'll keep an eye on the place for us?"

Caleb nodded, chewing a bite of his beefsteak.

"How long do you think you'll be gone?" he asked.

"Five days," Rab said. "Three to get there, two to get back."

In truth, Rab Sinclair was no cattleman. He preferred to wander more than a cattleman could afford to do. His herd was small, far smaller than his valley ranch could have supported. His real love of the ranch wasn't in the cows but in the small herd of mustangs that roamed his valley. He said often that the valley belonged to those mustangs, and he was just occupying their ground.

"Are just the two of you going?" Caleb asked.

"Vazquez is coming with us," Rab said.

Caleb nodded.

"I ain't surprised by that," he said. "Last I seen him, a week or two ago, he was asking if you were planning any drives."

Vazquez was a part time deputy sheriff for San Miguel County, though lately he'd been hiring on for ranch work more than he'd been sheriffing. Vazquez built a reputation for being handy with a gun. Early in his career as a deputy sheriff, Vazquez found himself in a shoot 'em up with a couple of wanted men. He killed both of them. About a year later, a drunk in town went for his gun, and Vazquez drew first and drilled the drunk through the neck.

After that, Sheriff Juan Romero put Vazquez on tax collection duty. He spent most of his time as a deputy sheriff riding out to remote ranches and settlements in San Miguel County serving notice of tax delinquency. It wasn't that Sheriff Romero didn't want Vazquez shooting anybody else, but some of the ranchers took exception to tax collections. Romero figured they'd be less likely to take a shot at a deputy sheriff with a reputation.

But Vazquez didn't like collecting taxes any more than folks liked paying them, and so he took other work when he could find it with a view to leaving the sheriff's office one day.

"Kuwatee is going, too," Rab said.

That was also no surprise. A half-breed Apache, Kuwatee was another of what Rab called "Evangeline's strays."

Evangeline sometimes took in folks who were going through a rough patch or suffered from a perpetual run of bad luck.

When Rab talked of "Evangeline's strays," Caleb knew that he was one, too.

Kuwatee was a half-breed Apache, though no one was quite sure what the other half was. Maybe white, or maybe Mexican. Either way, he had no people. He wasn't accepted among the Apache people, he wasn't trusted by the whites or the Mexicans. So Kuwatee existed on his own.

About the only person Kuwatee trusted was Rab Sinclair, because Rab knew what it was like to be of two worlds.

Rab called them "Evangeline's strays," but Caleb figured they all belonged as much to Rab as they did Evangeline.

There were others, too, who came and went. Sometimes women from town came and lived in the cabin when their husbands were on a drunk and feeling violent. Sometimes drifters who needed work and knew Rab. Sometimes Indians, especially from the Ute People. Sometimes they were men who were on the run from the law, but because Rab knew them he'd take them in.

It was fine for Rab to blame all the strays on Evangeline, but Caleb thought he knew better.

When they showed up, Rab would pay them something to work. Some would get tired of the work and drift on. Others would save up their wages and move on when they were back on their feet or thought they'd out-waited the law.

Kuwatee never moved on, though.

Caleb seldom saw him around the ranch, and he only ever seemed to do any work when Rab was driving cattle to one of the forts or to market.

A five-day cattle drive meant they were just driving fifty head of cattle to Fort Union, and if they pushed the trip could be done in four days. Rab and Evangeline made the drive up to Fort Union once every couple of months, and Rab always was slow coming back. A good horse could easily get back from Fort Union in a day, but Rab Sinclair liked to meander. He'd ride up toward the mountains or ride east a ways toward the Canadian River.

"These fellers you're running around with," Rab said. "Any of them work?"

"They work," Caleb said.

"That boy Chavez that came at me, he's been trouble his whole life."

"He's a friend of mine," Caleb said.

"He's a loafer, and I wouldn't be surprised if he's not a thief, to boot."

Caleb frowned.

"They're my friends," he said. "Chavez is kind of dumb, but he's not a bad person."

"What do you mean he came at you?" Evangeline asked.

"It was nothing," Rab said. "He thought he wanted to fight, and I showed him that he didn't."

Caleb chuckled, but caught himself and stopped quickly. He was feeling raw toward Rab, just now, but he could not help but admire the man. And the memory of the way Rab put Chavez on the ground made him grin in spite of himself.

"And that other feller, Matty Rio. Where does he work that he affords clothes like that?"

Caleb shrugged.

"He works around at different places," Caleb said.

"Let's not worry so much about it right now," Evangeline interrupted. "Caleb's a smart young man, and he's capable of choosing the company he spends time with."

Rab curled his bottom lip and bit it, giving a slight shake to his head. But he glanced at Evangeline and winked at her.

"Yes, ma'am," he said. "The only other thing I'll say about it is this. Caleb, if you keep running around with these fellas, you're headed for a violent outcome. They're ne'er-do-wells of the worst sort. I've seen their sort plenty of times, and they'll lead you down a bad path."

Caleb took another bite of food, grateful that Evangeline had put an end to the interrogation.

After supper, he sat for a while on the cabin porch with Rab and Evangeline.

Rab smoked his pipe and Evangeline watched the stars overhead, and none of them said much of anything.

But Caleb Morgan thought hard about how he wanted something else from life than living on Rab Sinclair's ranch. The others his age got up to rowdy fun in the saloons. They knew something of the women who worked the upstairs rooms. They wore fine clothes and enjoyed their lives.

Here, on this ranch, Caleb was beginning to feel that life was passing him by, and he wanted to catch up to it.

***

"I thought you wanted me to talk to him about the company he's been keeping," Rab said after Caleb had gone back down to his cabin.

"I do," Evangeline said. "But you shouldn't make him feel like you're accusing him of something."

The cabin sat down below the straight cliffs of a low mesa, and above it there was a large stand of ponderosa pines. The scent of them drifting down on an evening breeze in late spring was a thing that Evangeline loved. It reminded her sometimes of her childhood home on the American River.

Thinking about California brought back memories of when she was around Caleb's age, maybe even a little younger.

"Not having the perspective of experience, a young person is bound to make some poor choices. But pride, especially the pride of youth, sometimes prevents a fair judgment on those choices. In the end, what will matter most to any of us is that the choices we make are our own."

Evangeline thought of how her father objected and her mother cried when she decided to marry a man and move to Santa Fe. It was not pleasant, but in the end her parents acquiesced not because they came to believe in the wisdom of the choice but because it eased their burden.

When her husband died and she found herself penniless in Santa Fe, without even money enough to go back to California, Evangeline had to make her way as best she could. In the end, she could look back now and understand the path she was on. Poor choices and bad luck led her into a rough patch, but she came out of that rough patch better and happier than she ever thought she could be.

"It will work out for Caleb," Evangeline said. "Don't

you think?"

The bowl of Rab's pipe grew orange and bright for a moment, and smoke billowed from the corner of his mouth.

"That boy Chavez is an idiot," Rab Sinclair said. "And I don't like the look of that other one. What did Caleb say his name was?"

"Matty Rio," Evangeline reminded him.

"What kind of fool name is that?" Rab said. "Where's he come from? How's he make his living? There ain't many people in New Mexico Territory who I don't know or haven't heard of, but I've never heard of him."

Evangeline laughed.

"Oh, Rabbie, there are tens of thousands of people in New Mexico Territory you've never heard of."

Sinclair grinned and drew on his pipe again, lighting his face a little in the glow of it. Evangeline grinned to see that he was grinning.

"There's bad sorts, Evangeline," Rab said. "I don't have to tell you that. I found you working in a saloon in Santa Fe. I reckon you've seen plenty of it yourself. Poor choices are one thing, but if a boy like Caleb falls in with bad sorts, they could lead him far astray."

Evangeline frowned.

"Caleb's a good boy," she said.

"I ain't saying he's not," Rab said.

"You said 'a boy like Caleb.' What do you mean by that?"

Rab pondered the question. For him, things were plain to see but sometimes more difficult to put into words.

"He ain't anchored," Rab said. "He drifts, and when a thing drifts it's not hard for it to be caught by the current and swept away. Without his folks to anchor him, Caleb goes where the current takes him. When we came along, the current brought him with us. But now he's at an age where he's taken an interest in things outside of what he's known, and those interests are a new current taking him off in a different direction."

Rab stood up from his rocking chair and banged the bowl of his pipe against the porch railing to knock out the burnt ashes. The cracks of the pipe against the rail echoed in the valley.

"I don't mean to say he's moving from one place to another," Rab said. "I mean drifting and being swept by the current in terms of his values and things he holds important."

Evangeline wondered.

"Did you drift with the current when you were his age?"

Rab chuckled.

"Not hardly," he said. "I've always known pretty well who I was."

He dug the pipe into his tobacco pouch, thumbing tobacco into the bowl, and he struck a match to relight it.

"But even so, I made some poor choices when I was about Caleb's age," Rab said. "I was doing a job for a man, working as a guide. I let that man influence me some. I knew what was right and what needed to be done, but I went along with what he said because he was older and he was the one paying the wages. And when you're young like that, it's sometimes hard to stand up for what you think."

Evangeline knew there were things in his past that he wouldn't talk about with her, and she knew Rab had said just about as much as he cared to about this. He had a way about him, when he got wistful and thinking back on past days.

"I paid for heeding bad advice, but the man that gave me that advice, he paid more."

A silence settled in between them for a long time. Evangeline sat still and watched the stars from under the lip of the porch roof. Rab leaned against the railing of the porch, drawing on his pipe, and looking out through the darkened valley with a thought to catching sight of the mustangs. But there wasn't much of a moon, and the juniper bushes all through the valley limited the view quite a bit.

Evangeline found it hard sometimes to imagine Rab Sinclair's life before she came into it. She knew how he was raised, living among the various Tribes People with his father. She knew when he was about Caleb's age, he had led wagon trains along the Santa Fe Trail and that he had been a scout in the War for a while before he grew weary of it, in the way that he sometimes did.

But she couldn't imagine a time when someone else could impose his will on Rab Sinclair. The man she knew was stubborn and decisive.

Not for the first time, Evangeline wondered if he had loved some other woman.

"We should turn in," Rab said. "Kuwatee and Vazquez will be here at sunup expecting to cut out the steers and start north by early afternoon. We don't want to still be abed when they get here."

- 2 -

Matty Rio kicked his boots up on the table in the saloon and leaned back in his chair.

The boots were black and polished to a shine, and the man didn't look like he'd seen a speck of trail dust in all his life. He wore a pearl-handled Colt Army tucked into a red sash tied around his waist.

A couple of the guys had put a dirty dishrag that Hank Little used to wipe up spilt liquor against Chavez's head to stop the bleeding, and they'd cinched it into place with a leather belt. Chavez looked absurd, and he'd been the butt of many jokes all evening.

"Laugh all you want to, but I'm going to kill that bastard Rab Sinclair," Chavez said.

"Hell you will," Matty Rio said. "He's a tough hombre and would do for you ten times over before you ever could get a drop on him."

Regardless of Caleb Morgan's protestations that none among his crowd was older than the rest, Matty Rio was twenty-eight years old. Like Rab, he had a hard time seeing Chavez and Caleb as men. They seemed like boys to him.

But Matty Rio knew that boys could be impressed with someone like him. A fine dresser, tall and good looking. Matty possessed a cocksure attitude that he wore in his walk and his talk, and the result was that boys trying hard to become men tended to respect him and follow him. Men, of course, saw him for what he was.

There were six of them altogether, with Caleb Morgan being the sixth and newest addition.

There was Bud Woolery, who'd been with Matty Rio the longest. Matty met Woolery up in Trinidad. His father was an old man when Bud was born, a trapper and a hunter from the old days who was mean like a rattlesnake. Bud's daddy used to beat on him regular, and Bud grew up to be mean like his daddy. Woolery's favorite thing was shooting dogs and cats, and because of it, Bud Woolery was a pretty fair shot with his Remington six-shooter. Wool wore an old buckskin jacket that had been his father's and was too big for him and it was worn out at the elbows.

Wool, as they called him, was dangerous because everything he did was on impulse without a moment's consideration.

Union Joe was the one Matty Rio counted on the most.

No older than any of the others, Union Joe seemed far more mature. Union Joe was a deserter from the US Army. He'd been a private at Fort Union, but he got tired of being ordered around and told what to do, so one night he slipped past the guard on a stolen cavalry horse.

He rode north, and in Trinidad he abandoned the horse and spent the last of what he had on some clothes. He had no skills at making a living, so he turned to stealing, and Union Joe nearly got himself shot when he was caught. He made a run, and that's when he fell in with Bud Woolery. Wool brought him to Matty Rio, and Union Joe joined the loose affiliation to make it a threesome.

But Matty Rio was looking for an outfit of six for what he had in mind.

On the road to Canon City they held up a traveler. The traveler turned out to have a mite of courage and went for his gun, but Bud Woolery put him down like he would have any other dog.

Having committed murder in addition to robbery, Matty Rio decided getting the outfit out of Colorado Territory was the smart play. So they returned to Trinidad and then quickly dropped south to Las Vegas.

That's where they met Chavez and his pal Eduardo.

Chavez and Eduardo didn't have anything going, so they took up with Matty Rio and the others. Matty rented a room above a store with the money they took off the murdered traveler, and all five of them had been living in that room for three months.

They met Caleb Morgan in Hank Little's saloon when Caleb was in town getting supplies for the ranch. He'd driven the buckboard in to get sacks of flour and sugar and other things Evangeline wanted, but he'd decided he was old enough to walk into a saloon and order a beer if he wanted to.

Caleb knew that Hank Little was friends with Rab Sinclair, so he figured Hank Little's saloon was okay to walk into.

Chavez, who recognized Caleb from around town, started teasing him because Chavez had four men backing him.

Caleb ignored him. He sat facing Hank who was behind the bar, his straight back directed at Chavez and the others sitting at the table with him.

And then Chavez kicked the barstool out from under him.

Caleb spilled onto the floor, but he came up with a knife at Chavez's throat, and that's the moment when Matty Rio knew he'd found the sixth member of his outfit.

Caleb Morgan took some courting. They didn't even see him for another week, but the next time he was in town Matty Rio bought him a drink, and then another. And that went on for a while, until soon Caleb was coming to town regularly to see Matty and the other boys.

Now Matty Rio had his gang put together and all that was left was to start making plans.

"Besides, you might as well forget about Rab Sinclair. In a month we'll be long gone from here and rolling in so much money you won't care about a little knock to the head."

"A month?" Chavez asked.

Only once in his life had Chavez been up to Fort Union, and that was the farthest he'd ever gone. Matty Rio was talking about California, and the thought of it both excited and frightened him. But the thought of it coming soon tended to tip the scales toward fear.

"A month from now we'll be on our way to California, and done with this penny-ante town," Matty Rio said.

Union Joe snorted.

"We better get a big haul in this holdup," he said. "Cause we'll be needing to replace a whole lotta shoe leather if we're walking all the way to California."

"Who's walking?" Matty Rio laughed. "Chavez, for one, ain't walking. Are you, big fella?"

Matty dropped his feet and slapped Chavez on his fat belly.

Chavez laughed despite the pain in his head and the sharpness of the smack on his stomach. He liked Matty Rio and didn't mind becoming the butt of a joke only as long as it was just the guys in the outfit doing the laughing. For the first time in his life, Chavez felt like he had people who belonged to him. Real friends. They did not care about his dead father in the mountains nor the race of his mother, and though they teased him a bit about it.

Union Joe didn't laugh with the rest of them. He leaned forward toward Matty Rio.

"What are we going to do? Hold up the stagecoach and then ask them to give us passage to California?"

"We're going to have horses," Matty said. "Chavez, who did you tell me has some of the best horses around

Las Vegas?"

Chavez grinned and touched the bandage on his head.

"Rab Sinclair's remuda is one of the best around," he said. "Strong horses that can go all day."

Union Joe shook his head.

"I don't see how that does us any use at all," he said. "He ain't the sort that we just stride onto his ranch and steal his horses."

Matty Rio grinned.

"Maybe not," Matty said. "But Caleb Morgan lives on Rab Sinclair's ranch, and that's our way into the ranch."

- 3 -

Since the war, Las Vegas had become one of the most important towns in New Mexico Territory for commerce. Its position on the Santa Fe Trail meant that most of the goods flowing into New Mexico Territory or even those headed for Mexico City came through here. Rab Sinclair, working as a guide on the Santa Fe Trail, had come through Las Vegas a number of times and liked the place.

During the War, Rab Sinclair spent a little time as a scout for the Rebels, but when he started thinking about killing or being killed over another man's politics, he decided to ride away from it and go live among the Ute People in the San Juan Mountains.

After the war, he settled in Las Vegas.

He worked a number of jobs for a year or two, mostly guarding freight shipments from Las Vegas to Santa Fe.

Rab never intended to become a rancher. It did not much suit his preferences. But he knew an old rancher who was among the first to claim land after the territory went to the United States in '48, and when the rancher grew homesick and decided to move back to Kentucky, he sold a piece of his ranch east of Las Vegas to Rab for a good sum. The man essentially gave Rab the cattle and only charged him for the land.

The ranch had good water, a rarity in those parts, and Rab liked the way it was situated down in a long valley. So he paid the meager price and went into the ranching business.

Though the work was hard, there wasn't much to it. The cattle were hardy and there was plenty of forage. The valley meant that Rab seldom had to worry about wandering steers. He struck a deal to sell beeves to the quartermaster at Fort Union, and then to the quartermaster at Fort Craig. He also sold cattle a few times at Fort Sumner for the Apache and Navajo reservation before it was abandoned. But other than driving the cattle, Rab found that the responsibilities of ranching were neither arduous nor time consuming. He had plenty of opportunity to ride the blue roan up into the mountains overlooking Las Vegas and to ride down through the Pecos Valley, almost completely deserted of people at the time.

But the ranch held him in place more than he liked.

"Cut out the fattest steers," Rab said.

Kuwatee and Vazquez were both good hands for ranch work because they were skilled on the back of a horse. Vazquez came from a family of vaqueros, and though he was more metropolitan these days, he'd grown up working cattle with his uncles and father. Kuwatee, for his part, was only half Apache, but it was the horse-riding half.

The work to draw fifty cattle from the herd could be finished in a couple of hours. Vazquez and Kuwatee cut them out in twos and threes, and Evangeline and Rab pushed them farther up the valley to keep them separated.

They worked fast and did not spare the horses. When the cutting out was finished, they would get new mounts and spares for the ride to Fort Union. A long drive required a wagon to haul supplies, but they were only driving these cattle about forty miles. A couple of pack mules and their saddlebags would carry all the gear they needed.

While Rab and the others gathered the cattle for the drive, Caleb Morgan rounded up the horses they would take.

Rab was saving Cromwell, the blue roan, for the drive. Evangeline would ride her preferred buckskin. Vazquez and Kuwatee had their own horses, but they would ride a couple from Rab's remuda.

While Caleb caught horses out of the pasture and brought them into the barn, it occurred to him that anyone who spent much time looking over Rab's ranch wouldn't take long to determine that the man's passion was in horses and not cattle.

Rab had fine horses. Quarter horses and

Appaloosas, a couple of gaited horses, a dozen good paints, and a number of draft horses. He kept stallions and broodmares. He traded and sold horses some, but he tended to be particular about who he would sell a horse to. Most all of them were good saddle horses, but they tended to all have too many eccentricities. The truth was, Rab spoiled his horses, and that was why a herd of strong mustangs still ran wild on his place. All of those horses could have been broke and turned into cash money, but Rab liked to let them run.

By late morning Caleb had the horses and pack mules in the barn and ready to go. Kuwatee and Vazquez showed up first to get fresh mounts while Rab and Evangeline started the herd of steers up out of the valley. When the hired hands were mounted and rode out, Rab and Evangeline came back in to get their fresh mounts and the rest of the horses and the pack mules.

And then they were gone.

Caleb was alone and in charge of the ranch for the next few days.

He saddled a big bay and rode into town.

- 4 -

Matty Rio didn't mind to start drinking early, and by the time Caleb Morgan rode into town the outfit was in its usual spot in Hank Little's saloon.

"Sorry about that last night," Caleb told Chavez.

The belt was gone, in favor of a strip of cheesecloth tied around his head, but Chavez still looked absurd.

"Ain't no reason to apologize to him," Union Joe said. "All that was his own fault."

Joe, who was younger than Matty Rio but more experienced for his brief service in the cavalry, knew something about life that the others did not. He had a respect for rough men and could recognize one on sight. He'd sorted out Rab Sinclair in a hurry as a man he did not want to fool around with.

Matty Rio seized on Joe's comment, but for his own purposes. He was courting Caleb Morgan and knew the boy could still go one way instead of the other.

"That's right," he said. "It ain't your fault at all, son. It's a lesson that Chavez earned. Ain't that right Chavez?"

Chavez merely grunted. His preference was that they not talk about it at all.

"The lesson, if you want to know, is that when a shotgun is settin' there on the table in front of you, maybe you ought not to go at a man with your fists."

Caleb, who had taken a seat across from Union Joe, shifted uneasily.

"You probably shouldn't go for your gun with Rab Sinclair, either," he said.

"He did draw that Dragoon pretty quick to bash Chavez in the head, didn't he?" Matty Rio said. "Anyway, ain't nobody here going to shoot Caleb's friend, and the other lesson Chavez learned is to leave that feller alone. Wool, go and get another round for everybody. As dry as it is out there, Caleb could use a beer."

Matty Rio handed Wool some coins to buy the drinks. He would have preferred to get Caleb a glass of whiskey, but there wasn't a lot of money left to be buying whiskey this early in the day.

"What we need to do is start talking business," Matty said. "This outfit needs to get into something profitable, and soon. Now, I happen to know for a fact that the stagecoach running between here and Santa Fe always has a strongbox that's loaded with cash and gold."

The others all knew that Matty was talking for Caleb's benefit. All of them, even Union Joe, already knew about the stagecoach and what Matty Rio planned to do.

"Wait now," Caleb said. "You're not talking about robbing a stagecoach?"

Matty grinned.

"Keep your voice down some," he said. "That money on the stagecoach is bank money, and stealing from the bank ain't like stealing from regular people. What I'm talking about is an easy play to get the money we need to get to San Francisco and get set up there."

Bud Woolery came back with the beers and set them on the table. Everyone reached for one except Caleb. Matty Rio could see Caleb's imagination working.

"What's the matter, son?" Matty asked. "Get your beer."

"Stealing, whether it's bank money or anyone else's, don't sit right with me," Caleb said.

Matty Rio laughed a little, not mocking the boy but in a careless way.

"I understand what you mean by that, Caleb. I sure do. Ain't nobody here a thief by nature, but let's be honest with each other. This outfit we've got, we don't hardly have two nickels to rub together. We all agree we're an outfit, and we all agree we want to get into something profitable together. Right?"

Caleb nodded his head.

"That's right, but I don't want to be involved in stealing money. From a stagecoach or a bank or anything else."

Matty nodded his head and smiled.

"Well, I can appreciate that, Caleb. I sure can."

Matty leaned back in his chair and looked at the ceiling.

"What else can we get into, boys, that might be profitable and make us enough money to get to California?"

All of them now mimicked Matty Rio, looking around thoughtfully.

"We could just go straight to a bank and rob that," Eduardo said.

Matty Rio laughed, and the others laughed. Caleb laughed, too, thinking Eduardo was making a joke.

"We could earn the money to get to California if we wanted to work as ranch hands for the next fifty years," Union Joe said. "But if we want to go while we're still young, we're going to have to think of something else."

"Well, that's right, ain't it," Matty Rio said. "If we want to seize on our youth, we've got to figure out something in a hurry."

If any of them had any idea what they were going to do when they got to California, Caleb Morgan hadn't heard them say. The outfit's plan, as far as he knew, was to get to California. That was something that appealed to Caleb. All he knew about California was that Evangeline had come up in California and that there was gold to be plucked from the rivers there. Even today, more than two decades since the first big strike, people were still making fortunes in California.

But no one had said anything about digging gold. No

one had said anything about doing anything. All the talk Caleb had heard was just about going to California.

The group sat in silence for some time, all of them making a show of concentrating on the problem at hand.

"I sure do understand your reluctance, Caleb. Surely, I do," Matty Rio finally said. "But I just don't see any other way for us to get the money we need and get it in a hurry."

"We could hire on with a freight company," Caleb suggested. "I know they've got wagons going to California regular."

"Well, we could do that," Matty said. "But we'd be in real luck if we found a company that would hire all of us. And I reckon they'd expect us to come back, at that. I don't know a freight company that sends its wagons off and don't care if they never see them again."

"The stagecoach is the only thing that makes sense," Chavez said. "Ain't no reason to argue about it."

"Well, it does make sense," Matty Rio said. "It would be an easy enough thing, if we did it right. Nobody gets hurt, and the only person out any money is the bank. That's about the best way I can think of for us to get the money we need to get to California."

Matty Rio watched Caleb to see if he looked like was convinced yet, but the boy had a disgusted expression.

"You didn't promise to be at supper tonight did you?" Matty said as a way to change the subject. "We don't have to worry about Rab Sinclair coming to fetch you again?"

"He's gone," Caleb said. "He took some cattle up to Fort Union."

Matty Rio glanced at Union Joe and gave him a grin. Caleb didn't know that they called Joe "Union" because he'd deserted from Fort Union.

"Gone on a cattle drive, huh?" Matty said. "How long does something like that take?"

"It should only take four days, but Rab won't be back for five. Maybe six if he feels like wandering farther than usual."

Matty Rio nodded his head thoughtfully.

If he wanted to make off with some of Rab Sinclair's horses, now would be the time to do it. His plans had been to use Caleb Morgan as a way to get onto the ranch and then to shoot Sinclair in the back. But this could be a lot easier than that. Stealing horses from a man who was days away on a cattle drive was the easiest thing in the world to do, especially when a partner in your outfit was the man left in charge of the horses.

"You look thirsty," Matty said to Caleb, tossing a half dollar to him. "Get yourself a whiskey."

***

"The thing I like about California is that a man can go there and be anything he wants," Matty Rio said. He spoke freely. This early in the afternoon, the only other person in the saloon was Hank Little, he and he was all the way over at the bar not paying any attention to them.

He stared off through the door of Hank Little's saloon, not looking at Caleb Morgan, but talking directly to him. The others had gone to beg an early supper off of Chavez's mother. To her distress, she'd become the cook for Matty Rio's outfit.

"It don't matter what you've done or never done, everything can start over in California. You want to go and be a rancher? They've got the prettiest valley ranch land you've ever seen. Get your cattle so fat you'll make a fortune every time you go to market with 'em. Or if you want to swing a pick and swirl a pan, there must be a thousand rivers and creeks with gold nuggets the size of your fist."

Caleb gave a skeptical frown.

"Don't believe me?" Matty Rio said. "I've seen 'em myself."

"You've been to California?"

"No, I ain't never have. But I've talked to prospectors who told it to me themselves. Boys that went to California to pan for gold, two years later they're on their way back east to home, made such a fortune they'll never work again."

Caleb licked his lips. It sounded appealing, though also unbelievable. He wondered what it would be like for a man to make a fortune so big in just two years that he'd never have to work again.

"San Francisco is as fine a city as any they have in Europe. And they've got the prettiest gals in San Francisco like you wouldn't never see around here."

"I believe that," Caleb said.

Evangeline came from California, and she was the prettiest woman Caleb had ever seen. She didn't talk about gold nuggets the size of a fist, and she didn't talk about men making such a fortune in just two years, but Caleb had heard stories about fortunes being made in California and he did not have reason to doubt what Matty said.

"I think I'd like to try my hand at prospecting," Caleb said. "All I've done my whole life is work. If I could pan for gold and make so much that I wouldn't have to work but two years more, that'd be all right with me."

This was what Matty Rio had been waiting for. He just needed some sign from Caleb that there was something in California that interested him.

"Well, Caleb, that's the whole reason we're trying to get to California. The whole outfit wants to pan for gold."

Caleb nodded slowly, thinking about it.

"And maybe meet one of them San Francisco gals you were talking about."

"Yeah," Matty Rio said. "Gold and women. They're like partners. Once you've got some gold, you've got some women, too."

Caleb sighed heavily and shook his head.

"But you're talking about robbing a stagecoach to get there, and I can't be a part of that."

Matty nodded his head.

"I understand that," he said. "I know how you feel about that, and I don't disagree with you one bit. Except there ain't no other way for us to get the money to get out there. You've been working. Like you said, your whole life. Do you have money enough to go to California?"

"No," Caleb admitted.

"And Chavez," Matty Rio started laughing. "What do you think about Chavez, who ain't worked a day in his life? You think he's got money enough to go to California?"

"I wouldn't guess so," Caleb said.

"He ain't got money enough to see Hank Little at the bar over there," Matty Rio said. "I pay for every trip to the bar he makes. And it's not like we're talking about robbing the passengers. It's bank money, and I can tell you the honest truth is that the bank has plenty of money. Most of it stole off hard working folks, anyhow."

Caleb nodded. It was true. Even Rab didn't much trust banks. Not that he ever had much money, but when he did, he didn't like to put it in a bank.

"But Rabbie always says that there ain't no question about the right or wrong of stealing," Caleb said. "If it don't belong to you, don't take it. It's that simple."

Even as he said the words, Caleb heard himself and knew that he was mimicking Rab Sinclair. And when he said it to Matty Rio, who was far more sophisticated than Rab, the words sounded naive and childish.

"That's a good philosophy right there," Matty said. "I like that philosophy. But we're talking about bank money. And the way I see things, if it's money that was stole in the first place, then who's to say who it belongs to now?"

Caleb Morgan tried to work his way through the logic, but the twists and turns he had to make got to be too confusing. He wasn't sure that he could make sense of whether Matty Rio was right, but he also wasn't sure that he could point out where Matty was wrong.

Matty Rio had a way of talking to folks that made them come to his way of thinking. He always held back an ace-in-the-hole when he was trying to convince someone of something.

"You wouldn't even have to be there," Matty said. "You know what? Somebody's got to hang on to the horses for us. The way this works is we've got to have some spare horses. We hold up the stagecoach and then we have to get out fast. We'll run those horses pretty good for five or eight miles, and then we'll need spare horses. You could be our relay station."

Caleb nodded.

He didn't want to be involved in any stagecoach robbery, but he didn't so much mind the idea of holding spare mounts.

"Nobody's going to get hurt?" Caleb said.

"Why would anybody get hurt?" Matty Rio said. "We're not going to bother the passengers. And nobody is going to make a stand for bank money. They'll toss that strongbox off the stagecoach and be glad to go on their way."

Caleb thought about that. It made sense to him that if they didn't try to steal from the passengers nobody would risk their lives for the bank's money.

"And then we go on to California?" Caleb asked.

"That's right. We go on to California when it's finished."

Caleb took a heavy breath. He found it difficult to make a decision. He knew that what Matty Rio suggested was wrong, and yet the lure of a change in life was very strong.

It wasn't that Caleb didn't like Rab and Evangeline, and he was grateful to them. They'd been good to him. They took him in when, for the second time in his life, he was left with nobody. Rab paid him wages to do a job and seldom treated him like a child.

But Caleb yearned to be his own man, and he did not think that would ever happen while he was living on Rab

Sinclair's ranch in New Mexico Territory.

"All right," Caleb said.

Matty Rio grinned at him and slapped his hand inside Caleb's hand, giving it a good, firm shake.

"Partners," Matty Rio said. "I'm glad to hear it, Caleb. This outfit needs you, and I think you need this outfit. Now the only trouble we've got is getting some mounts."

- 5 -

Driving cattle up to Fort Union was about as easy a thing as a man could do other than sitting a rocking chair on a front porch.

Though they were not far from the Llano Estacado where bands of Comanche still roamed free and dangerous, this close to the fort – built for the sole purpose of protecting the Santa Fe Trail – they had nothing at all to fear from Indians of any sort. Neither would bandits be around to cause trouble. If they weren't moving cattle, they could be to the fort before dark, and bandits and Comanche did not operate a day's ride from cavalry.

The blue roan's easy gait suited Rab Sinclair.

He didn't much like following behind even a small herd of cattle. The dust they kicked up could choke a man. So Rab gave them space and picked up strays when he came across them.

The ride up to the fort followed grassland through easy, rolling hills. The mountains to the west were like a low, purple ribbon strung across the horizon. For most of the way to the fort, Rab could look over his left shoulder to see Hermit's Peak above Las Vegas and always know his way home. There were a few squat mesas that broke the horizon ahead of them, but Evangeline, riding out front of the herd and setting both the pace and the direction, could simply skirt the steers around those mesas.

Later, when they were closer to Fort Union, to the northeast Rab would be able to catch a glimpse of the Wagon Mound, so long as the day was clear.

"You remember that old mound, don't you Cromwell?" Rab said to the horse.

One of the last landmarks on the Santa Fe Trail before Las Vegas. It marked the end of the dry run of the trail, and more than once, Rab and Cromwell had seen the old Wagon Mound come up on the horizon as a salvation.

Water through here wasn't plentiful, but Evangeline knew the spots where they would have their best chance to find a creek for the animals. But it was still early spring, and while the days were plenty warm, the snow was clinging to the sides of the mountains, still, and there'd not yet been much rain to get water moving through the arroyos. If the creeks were dry, the animals would be fine, but they'd be less agreeable if they didn't have water.

Kuwatee was riding on the right flank of the herd,

just in Rab's sight. Vazquez was out on the left, easier to see. He might be able to catch sight of Evangeline from the top of a rise, but she was pushed ahead and the steers were kicking up such a dust that Rab could not now locate her.

Rab's greatest regret was on that Santa Fe Trail. A time when he was young and allowed himself to be governed by the man who was paying his wages, a professor traveling to California with his family, a Christian man whose religious beliefs led him to abhor violence. The man's beliefs cost him, and they cost Rab, too.

"But life has a way of working itself out," Rab said to the horse.

Like any man who spends more time with his horse than he does with people, Rab had a habit of talking to Cromwell, and these conversations had given him to believe that the horse understood every bit of what he was thinking.

Cromwell stretched his neck and yawned, his big teeth jutting forward. Rab reached out a hand and rubbed his neck.

"Am I boring you?" Rab laughed. "Close that big ol' mouth."

The sun was already getting near to touching the mountains in the west, and that meant that by now Evangeline was probably finding a place to set camp for the night. Somewhere near to a creek where the cattle would have a natural barrier and might not wander. They'd only managed seven or eight miles in the afternoon, but it was better not to push the steers too hard. Rab didn't want them to lose any weight, even on a short drive. Let them eat all the way to the fort and they'd be just as fat as when they started, and good fat steers meant that he'd keep getting contracts from the quartermaster at Fort Union.

After a little while, Kuwatee waved his hat over his head.

Evangeline had found a campsite down in a hollow by a creek. Rab recognized the spot. They'd camped here before. A line of cottonwoods traveling the route of the hollow showed that the arroyo probably had water through at least some of the year, and Rab hoped there was good water in it now. It was always better to have water for the livestock, even if the camp was just seven or eight miles from home, but he really wanted to wash some of the dust off of his face.

Vazquez and Kuwatee helped Rab push the cattle down into the hollow where they'd stay overnight so long as a coyote didn't spook them. When that was finished, he rode the blue roan down into the hollow.

With just four of them driving the cattle, Evangeline kept the remuda and the pack mules with her. The horses followed along without any trouble, all of them smart enough to know their job on these cattle drives. The mules were on a tether that Evangeline led, and other than the occasional tug she didn't have to do much with them.

By the time the steers were down in the hollow, Evangeline had strung a line between a couple of the big cotton woods to picket the horses. She'd already gathered wood for a campfire and was ready to heat up supper – beans and bacon with coffee.

"Any water in that creek?" Rab asked, riding the roan over to the other horses and dismounting.

"Dry as a bone," Evangeline said. "We're a couple of

months yet from enough rain to get it flowing."

"Too bad," Rab said. "I could stand a wash."

Evangeline grinned at him, watching him take the saddle off the blue roan.

"Trailing steers is dirty work, Rabbie," she said. "I expect you won't need a plate of supper, though, with all that dust you ate today."

Rab grinned at her as he hitched Cromwell to the rope that Evangeline had strung between the cottonwoods.

He used his bandanna to knock off as much dust as he could, and then he took a seat by the fire.

Kuwatee rode in and ate while Vazquez continued to ride watch on the cattle. When he was finished eating, Kuwatee would change mounts, and take the first night watch. Mostly the night watch existed simply to keep coyotes away. The steers would stray some, even though they'd pushed them into the hollow. Come morning, they would have to get the herd back together. But none of the steers would stray too far, and with such a small number of cattle the job of getting them going come morning would be quick enough.

"I wonder if we should have brought Caleb," Evangeline said, taking a forkful of beans and bacon.

"Small herd," Rab said. "The four of us can manage it fine."

"I wasn't thinking about that," she said.

"You're thinking about those fellas he's running around with?" Rab asked.

"You've seen them," Evangeline said. "What did you think of them?"

"Only ones I know are Chavez and Eduardo, and they're a couple of loafers," Rab said.

"But you saw the others," Evangeline said. "What did you think of them?"

Rab grinned at Evangeline. Though they'd lived together for a number of years, long enough that everyone who knew them took them to be husband and wife, they'd never talked much about children – whether they wanted children or should have them. Rab always figured that sooner or later Evangeline would fall pregnant, though he found it hard to imagine her as a mother. But it had not happened yet.

He knew that sometimes women were barren and could not have children, and when he gave it any thought at all, he wondered some if maybe Evangeline was unable to conceive. Because of that, he seldom said anything to her about motherhood.

But now he broke that habit.

"You ain't his mama," Rab said. "We've always agreed that we would give him space to grow into a man because he's old enough to do that."

Evangeline laughed.

"Oh, hell, Rabbie, all I did was ask what you think of the boys he's running around with."

Rab scraped his fork across his plate, taking a last bite of his beans. He didn't answer her right away.

Kuwatee ate silently, listening to the conversation. He generally liked Caleb Morgan, as much as he liked anyone. But he did not meddle in other people's affairs. If Caleb Morgan was running with some boys who were trouble, that was Caleb Morgan's problem.

"They're no good," Rab said. "That's my impression. The one that's kind of the pack leader, he's the sporty one with the clean clothes. I don't remember now what Caleb said his name is."

"Matty Rio," Evangeline said.

"I've seen his sort before. I'd peg him as a thief. There's another one, a bit older than Caleb, maybe. He deserted from the army."

"He told you that?" Evangeline asked.

"No. He's wearing army issue boots. If he didn't desert, then he killed a cavalryman and took his boots. But I don't think he has the look of a killer. But I look at them, and I see trouble. They don't have any kind of work, which means they're keeping their eyes open for easy ways to get money. I make them out to be thieves or worse."

Kuwatee stood up.

"I'm going to relieve Vazquez," he said.

Rab nodded to him. He fished into his pocket for his pipe and tobacco.

"Surely Caleb wouldn't get involved in anything like that," Evangeline said, though she wasn't sure if she was asking a question or making a statement.

"I would hope not," Rab said.

"What happens if he does?" Evangeline said.

"Then it's like I said to him last night at supper. If Caleb gets involved with those fellas and gets into some sort of thieving, he's is setting himself up for a lot of trouble. Those boys don't strike me as being smart enough to run very far from the law. But Caleb is smart, and he was brought up with good examples. You have to trust the boy to make good choices."

***

Vazquez had the middle watch, and he woke Rab Sinclair in the early morning hours, well before dawn. The temperature dropped quite a bit, and it was cold for the drovers sleeping under the stars. Rab found he was stiff from the ground.

"Every drive seems to be harder," he said, stretching out the kinks and keeping his voice low so as not to disrupt the others still asleep.

Because they didn't have a wagon and only pack mules, they didn't even bring decent bedrolls. Just a couple of worn blankets for each of them.

"You're getting soft, old man," Vazquez teased him. They were not so different in age, but to a man still in his twenties, a man in his thirties seemed a great deal older.

Before waking Rab, Vazquez put a fresh pot of coffee on the fire, and Rab now wrapped a blanket over his shoulders and walked to the fire to get a cup.

"Any trouble?"

"Didn't even hear a coyote howl the whole night," Vazquez said.

They'd not had much opportunity to talk, the previous day's work always keeping them separate. But Rab was curious to find out what Vazquez might know about Matty Rio and his gang.

"I've seen them around town," Vazquez said. "He's that fancy dresser, right? Hanging around Hank Little's place and spending time with fat Chavez."

"That's right," Rab said.

Vazquez shrugged.

"I can't say I know anything about them. The sheriff hasn't said anything to me. If he's wanted, he's making it easy to find him."

"Matty Rio," Rab said. "I would guess that ain't the name he was born with."

Vazquez chuckled.

"Probably not. But unless there's something I don't know, he hasn't caused any trouble around town."

"You formed an impression of him?" Rab asked.

Vazquez grunted.

"You taught me something, Rab, when I first became a lawman. Do you remember what you told me about watching out for myself and keeping safe?"

Rab thought about it. He knew he had a habit of dispensing advice, but he often forgot the specifics of the advice dispensed.

"Remind me," Rab said.

"You told me that every time you walk into a crowded room you look around and pick out the person in that room you'll have to kill first."

Rab chuckled as he took a sip from his coffee.

"Yep," he said. "That's sage wisdom. If it goes wrong, it's always good to know ahead of time where to aim when you draw."

"Well, if I walk into a room and Matty Rio is in there, he's the first one getting shot if it goes wrong. That's the impression I've formed."

Rab nodded, taking another drink from the coffee. It helped to warm him a little, or at least not feel so bad about the cold.

"Go and get some sleep," Rab said. "Dawn'll come early and we'll need to head on."

- 6 -

The walk out to Rab Sinclair's ranch took longer than Matty Rio realized it was going to. It was made worse because Chavez couldn't go farther than a mile without having to find a rock to sit on. At last Matty Rio got sick of the delays and told Chavez to just catch up when he could catch up. He left Wool and Eduardo behind to keep an eye on Chavez and took Union Joe with him. But then Matty and Joe got lost, missing the cut to Sinclair's ranch completely.

So it was late in the afternoon when Matty Rio and Union Joe were finally walking a path from the road to

Sinclair's ranch.

Caleb Morgan was at the barn near the houses mucking out one of the stalls when he caught sight of two people walking the ranch. Even from a distance he could see that one of them was Matty Rio – nobody in Las Vegas, or all of New Mexico Territory, so far as Caleb knew, dressed like Matty Rio.

Caleb walked from the barn and waved to the visitors, meeting them halfway.

"Almost didn't find you," Matty Rio said.

"Did you walk all the way from town?" Caleb asked.

"You don't see no horses, do you?" Matty Rio said, irritated at the question but trying to keep a level tone. "Have Wool and the others showed up yet?"

"I haven't seen 'em," Caleb said.

"Well, look here, let's get somewhere that we can sit down and maybe have a glass of whiskey."

Caleb frowned.

"I can help you with a seat, but I don't keep no bottles here."

The three of them made their way toward Caleb's cabin.

"What about your pal Rab Sinclair?" Matty Rio asked. "He got a bottle in his cabin?"

Caleb knew that Rab kept some liquor in his cabin, though he seldom saw Rab take a drink.

"He's got some bottles, but that's really Rab's whiskey. I don't think he'd want me going into his cabin and taking it."

Matty Rio didn't care for the answer and cut his eyes at Caleb.

"You've got guests," he said. "Surely Sinclair wouldn't want you to have guests over and not offer 'em something to drink."

Caleb Morgan didn't want to disappoint his new friends, nor did he want to seem like a boy who didn't have access to whiskey. He could pay Rab for the bottle, or even buy a bottle from Hank Little to replace it.

"I'll go and get a bottle," he said. "Y'all can have a seat there on the porch of my cabin."

Caleb changed direction to walk down to Rab's cabin while Matty Rio and Union Joe walked on to his cabin.

What perplexed Caleb was how Matty Rio and Union Joe just showed up at the ranch without horses or a buggy or anything. It was a long walk from town, and even if they started back now, they probably wouldn't make it back before dark. It gave him an odd feeling to think that they might be planning to stay the night.

Inside, Caleb found three bottles of whiskey in a cabinet. One of them was opened, and Caleb skipped past that one, knowing how much Matty and Joe could drink at a sitting. He got one of the full bottles and went back out to his cabin. Caleb's cabin sat beyond the barn. It had been Rab's idea that Caleb's cabin shouldn't be too close to give the young man a sense that he had his own place.

By the time Caleb got back to his cabin, Matty Rio had his boots and socks off his feet and was examining one of his heels.

"Damn if I don't have a blister," he said. "I like them boots, but they ain't broke in good a'tall."

"I'll get a couple of cups," Caleb said.

"Don't worry about it," Matty Rio said, reaching for the bottle. "We'll drink from this."

Matty took off his hat and tossed it down on a table that Evangeline had made for Caleb. It was made from sticks woven together like cloth.

Matty had long, brown hair that somehow kept a wave even under his hat. The man was a true marvel of style and sophistication, even sitting there drinking whiskey straight from a bottle with his boots and socks off, Caleb still thought the man was someone to admire.

Matty had made it pretty clear that he had an easy way with women when there were women to be found, and when Caleb was in his company, Caleb liked to watch Matty to try to mimic his behavior.

Caleb leaned against the railing on the cabin and watched Matty Rio wince as he touched the blister on his ankle.

"If you'd wear boots that didn't shine so much, you might not get them blisters," Union Joe said.

To prove the point, he stretched out his own boots. Joe's boots were black and made of leather, and they covered his shins all the way up to his knees. But they were well broken with creases where his ankle bent.

"Those look like cavalry boots," Caleb said.

Union Joe glanced at him.

"I didn't know you was in the army," he said.

"Well, I ain't," Caleb said. "But we've drove cattle up to Fort Union and down to Fort Craig, and I've seen plenty of cavalry boots."

"They're good boots," Union Joe said.

"Course, in the army you'd have to keep a shine on 'em," Caleb said, noting that inside the creases the boots were covered in a layer of dirt.

"You gotta do a lot of things in the army," Union Joe said. "Most of them things I ain't interested in doing."

There was a tone to Joe's voice that made Caleb decide not to talk about the boots any further.

"So what are y'all doing out here?" Caleb asked.

"We come to see you, Caleb," Matty Rio said, leaving the blister for a moment. "Chavez and Eduardo and Wool are on their way, but Chavez is too slow so we left them back yonder some."

"What did you come to see me about?" Caleb asked.

Matty took a swig from the bottle and handed it over to Joe.

"What we talked about last night," Matty said. "We need to make plans if we're going to do this thing."

"I was going to come to town," Caleb said. "I just needed to finish some chores here."

Matty shrugged.

"It's easier to talk here, ain't it? Don't have Hank Little cocking his ear toward us."

As they spoke, Matty Rio took sight of Chavez and the others coming along the trail through the valley.

"Well there they are," he said. "You watch this. Chavez is going to have to sit and take another rest even before he gets here. Me and Joe got lost – walked right on past this place – and still managed to turn around and get back here way ahead of them."

Chavez, Wool, and Eduardo offered a few minutes of entertainment while the others watched to see if Chavez would have to sit again.

Their gait was slow enough, but Matty Rio was disappointed in his prediction as Chavez lumbered slowly up to the cabin.

Breathing heavy, he collapsed into a rocking chair.

"Ay, caramba," Chavez said between panting breaths. "I did not think I would ever make it here."

Matty Rio laughed at him and shook his head.

"We're going to need a draft horse to get him back to town," Matty said, with a glance at Caleb Morgan.

Caleb laughed, as did the others.

"No, I'm serious," Matty said. "You got any draft horses on this ranch?"

"Well, sure we do," Caleb said. "But those are Rab Sinclair's horses."

"But you can use 'em, right?"

Caleb thought about it. He had his own horse, but he also had the ability to saddle and ride any horse in Rab Sinclair's remuda. He never asked permission first, though there were a few horses he never touched. He wouldn't dream of riding Rab's blue roan, Cromwell. Neither would he ever ride the buckskin that Evangeline preferred.

But Caleb also wasn't sure that Rab wanted him loaning out a horse.

"I could harness a couple of horses to a wagon and drive all of you back to town, I reckon," Caleb said.

"Sure," Matty Rio said. "That would be fine."

He took a drink from the bottle and handed it over to Chavez.

"Let's talk about this job that's going to get us to California," Matty Rio said.

The smiles dropped from the faces of the outfit. They all knew now that it was finally time to get down to business. The others also knew that Matty intended to do this in a hurry, and that they'd come to the ranch to press Caleb Morgan into stealing a dozen horses from Rab Sinclair.

"A couple of weeks ago I rode the stagecoach to Santa Fe and then came back," Matty said. "I wanted to check it out and see how it was. There's two relay stops between here and Santa Fe. The first is down at Bernal Creek near Starvation Peak. The second is at the Pecos River. About twenty miles between each one."

Everyone in the outfit was familiar with the stops – even Eduardo and Chavez who had neither one been to Santa Fe. But still, the names of the places were familiar to them, and they knew the stagecoach made the stops.

"My thinking is that we want to catch the stagecoach about six miles after the Bernal Creek relay station."

No one said anything. None of them had ever robbed a stagecoach before, and they couldn't say if that was a good idea or a bad idea.

"Too close to the Pecos station, and they'll go that way for help. But if we're closer to the Bernal Creek station, they'll turn back for help."

"I would think they would drive right on to the next station," Union Joe interrupted.

"They won't be driving," Matty Rio grinned. "We're

going to take their team with us. When we've gone a ways, we'll cut the horses loose and let them wander. It buys us more time that way."

Union Joe nodded. He liked the thinking.

"So they'll walk back to Bernal Creek. At worst, it takes them about two hours to walk all the way back to the relay station. After two hours, we can be beyond the station at Pecos and nearly to Santa Fe. There ain't a telegraph at Bernal Creek, so they'll have to come all the way back to Las Vegas to telegraph ahead to Santa Fe. I figure that's another two hours by the time they get it done. With fresh horses, we can be all the way beyond Santa Fe when the sheriff here sends word to the sheriff there. We ride on to Albuquerque and lay low for a couple of days. We divide the haul from the stagecoach, and then we get on separate coaches for California."

"Separate coaches?" Chavez said. This was the first he'd heard of the gang splitting up, and he did not like it.

"When word gets out about the stagecoach robbery, they'll be looking for an outfit of five."

"Five?" Bud Woolery said. "We're an outfit of six."

Matty Rio nodded.

"Listen, Wool," Matty said. "Caleb is going to ride on ahead to just outside of Santa Fe with the fresh horses. Just the five of us are going to rob the stagecoach. So they'll be looking for five. But we'll split up in Albuquerque. We'll get stagecoaches on to California from there. I'm thinking we should go to San Francisco."

Nobody asked about horses or how an outfit with no horses was suddenly going to acquire a dozen.

"How much money do you reckon we're going to

get?" Union Joe asked.

Matty Rio smiled.

"What I've been told is that the stagecoach is going to have twenty thousand dollars on it," Matty said.

Caleb's mouth fell open. If he was to work fifty years on Rab Sinclair's ranch he wouldn't make twenty thousand dollars. It was a fortune unimaginable to the boy. For that matter, it was a fortune unimaginable to all of them.

But Caleb also could not imagine that the stage driver and shotgun rider would willingly let twenty thousand dollars in their care be taken.

"But nobody's going to get hurt?" Caleb asked.

"Of course nobody's going to get hurt," Matty Rio said. "Like I've done told you, Caleb. It's the bank's money. Nobody is going to risk his life for the bank's money."

"It just seems like a lot of money," Caleb said. "I can't hardly see anyone just letting you ride off with it."

Matty Rio shook his head and gave a mocking laugh.

"Look, Caleb, are you in this or ain't you? Are you with this outfit or not?"

Caleb swallowed hard. Up to now it had seemed like a child's game of imagining the future. But now, suddenly, it all seemed real. And he had a sense that whatever he said next was pivotal. Slowly, thoughtfully, he nodded his head. He could spend the rest of his life on Rab Sinclair's ranch working for a dollar a day, or he could go and see the world, maybe strike a fortune in the gold fields.

"I'm with this outfit," Caleb said.

"Good," Matty Rio said.

They sat quietly for some time, everyone giving thought to the plan.

Except for Caleb, the others had heard some or all of the plan already. Matty knew that Union Joe and Wool were with him whatever, and they both knew all of the plan. He knew that Chavez would balk at splitting up, so he'd waited until now to share that detail with him. Eduardo would go where Chavez went, so Matty wasn't worried about what complaints he might raise.

Now the question was just convincing Caleb to let them take Sinclair's horses.

That was going to be a delicate matter, and Matty Rio wanted to talk to Caleb about that without the others around, so he started putting his boots back on, wincing at the way the boots pressed against the painful blisters.

"Walk with me, Caleb," Matty Rio said, standing up and starting toward the barn.

***

"We're ready to go," Matty said. "The whole outfit is ready to do this. We've got a plan put together, and the stagecoach runs day after tomorrow."

"Day after tomorrow?" Caleb asked, surprised that it was so soon.

"The money is on the next stagecoach," Matty said. "That's the one that runs day after tomorrow."

"But Rab ain't back yet," Caleb said. "I told him I would watch the place while he's gone."

Matty Rio shook his head.

"What's to do to watch the place? Ain't nobody coming down here to steal cattle or horses. Hell, I was looking for the ranch and couldn't find it. The livestock all have water and grass. There ain't nothing to be done. Besides, how long until he gets back?"

"Three days," Caleb said. "Maybe four."

"That's plenty soon enough," Matty said. "This place will be all right if nobody's here for a couple of days."

Caleb shrugged. Matty was probably right. Rab had left the place completely unattended in the past when Caleb had helped him make the run up to Fort Union.

"The real problem we've got is that now is the time, if we're going to do it, tomorrow is the day we've got to get started. But we don't have any horses, Caleb."

Caleb nodded, thinking about it.

"Old Lou Anderson sells horses," Caleb said. "His place ain't far from here. He sells 'em cheap, too. I've seen him sell a horse for ten dollars that Rab said was a fifty dollar horse, easy."

Matty Rio bobbed his head from one shoulder to the next.

"That's a good suggestion, it surely is, but the problem we've got is that we couldn't buy a fifty dollar horse for fifty cents, Caleb. None of us have any money."

Caleb thought about it. "I've got about twenty dollars."

Matty Rio chuckled.

"That'll buy us two ten dollar horses from Lou Anderson," Matty said.

Caleb nodded.

"Listen, Caleb," Matty Rio said, dropping his voice to almost a whisper even though they'd walked far away from the others. "Now is when I need you to stand up and be a part of this outfit. I need you to help us make this happen. We need a dozen horses."

Caleb nodded, still not seeing what Matty was asking for.

"I don't know what I can do," Caleb said.

Matty Rio turned and waved a hand at the remuda in the fenced pasture.

"Go pick us out a dozen horses," Matty said. "Two of them need to be good draft horses that can tote Chavez."

Caleb Morgan's heart skipped a beat as he realized what Matty Rio was asking.

"You want to steal the horses from Rab?"

"Borrow them," Matty said. "Hell, when we get to Albuquerque, we'll send him six hundred dollars to pay for them. But we need horses, and you have horses here."

Caleb shook his head.

"I can't steal from Rab."

"He can get the horses back," Matty said. "We can send him enough money to buy the horses."

"I can't take Rab's horses," Caleb said. "Even if we pay him for them, it's stealing if he don't agree to the sale."

"He's got plenty of horses out here," Matty Rio said. "Look at all them horses. We'll pay him for the use and send him a letter to tell him where we've left them so he can get them back."

"Rab don't read," Caleb said.

Matty Rio laughed.

"He can find someone to read the letter to him," he said. "Lots of folks that don't read get letters."

"But it's stealing, and it's stealing from Rab Sinclair. You don't understand. He'd come after us."

"And we'll be gone," Matty Rio said.

Caleb looked at the horses in the pasture and remained quiet. The look of doubt stayed on his face, and Matty Rio was worried.

Matty had a fallback plan. If Caleb refused to take the horses, Matty intended to kill Caleb and take the horses himself. He liked the kid and thought Caleb could become a good member of the outfit. But he hadn't walked all the way out to this ranch to return empty handed. He was going to have those horses one way or another.

"They'll hang us for horse theft," Caleb said.

"Only if they catch us," Matty Rio said. "And if we give the horses back, and pay Sinclair for the use of them, then we won't even be stealing. But the point, Caleb, is that we've got to have horses, or everything we've been talking about is just talk. So why don't you go out there and pick out twelve good horses for us? You said you wanted to be part of this outfit, and we've got a problem that you can solve for us. I agreed to let you be our relay so you don't have to be there when we rob the stagecoach, but at some point, you've got to be willing to do your part for the rest of us."

Caleb started to make an argument, but then he stopped himself.

He realized that what Matty Rio said was true. Matty had made accommodations for Caleb based on his objections, and now Caleb felt pressure to do his part for the outfit.

"Twelve horses," Caleb said. "And we'll pay Rab for them when we get to Albuquerque."

"And we'll let him know where we've left the horses so that he can claim them if he wants," Matty Rio said.

"All right," Caleb said. "I'll pick them out."

- 7 -

Caleb Morgan did not sleep well. He wasn't even sure he'd slept at all.

He went to bed just after sunset with the intention of waking around midnight.

Through the evening hours, he could not get comfortable. The mattress on the bed seemed hard where he needed it to be soft and soft where he needed it to be hard. The chilly air of the evening came in through the open window, and Caleb pulled the blanket over him. Then he was too hot, and he kicked it off. The others slept on his floor, and it seemed that every time Caleb started to drift off to sleep someone would roll over and make some kind of noise. Chavez's snoring sounded like a cow choking on wet socks, and it went on for what seemed like hours.

At last it was midnight, and Caleb got out of bed. He woke up the others.

Eduardo took some meat from Rab Sinclair's smoke house and made ham and eggs for midnight meal while Caleb got the horses ready. He was riding his own horse and taking six more – one for each of them, including himself. He showed Matty Rio which horses he'd picked out for the rest of the gang.

Rab had plenty of spare saddles at the ranch that he kept for hands who hired on and did not have their own.

As Caleb helped Union Joe get those saddles and the rest of the horse tack, it occurred to him that he was not just stealing horses but also stealing the spare saddles and the rest of the gear. He even remembered the bottle of whiskey that went against his account.

A guilty conscience kept him focused on his work, even as the others laughed and cut up.

They ate, and by one-thirty in the morning, Caleb was leading six horses across the ranch and out toward the road.

Rab's ranch sat east and a little south of Las Vegas, so it was an easy journey to Bernal Creek where the stagecoach relay station was located. There was moon enough for Caleb to pick his way along the worn path that wound its way toward Starvation Peak.

The countryside was sandy and rocky and heavily dotted with juniper. In the dim light provided by the moon, the sandy path, wide enough for a wagon, glowed a silverish white while the juniper created dark walls of shadow on either side of the trail.

Caleb had stalled the horses before bed, and they were all willing enough to move and stretch their legs now that they were on the path. He had individual lead ropes for each horse so that if one spooked and bolted he wouldn't have a disaster. As he rode along, thinking about it, he realized this was a trick Rab Sinclair had taught him. He tied a loop on each individual lead on the inside horses, and then used a longer lead on the outside horses, running that longer lead through the loops of the inside horses. The inside horses were unlikely to spook, but if one of them on the outside decided to do something foolish, the others would not be dragged into the foolishness.

Thinking about it, Caleb realized that in the couple of years he'd worked and lived at Rab's ranch, he'd learned a lot, especially about caring for horses. Caring for cattle was less of a worry. That mostly consisted of dragging them out of muddy places in wet seasons and pushing them back to grassy pastures when they wandered too far. Other than that, the biggest part of caring for the cattle meant keeping the coyotes away.

But when it came to horses, Rab had an easy way with them, as he did with almost everything.

But it wasn't just horses. Rab taught Caleb to shoot. He taught Caleb to hunt. He taught him to read the signs of nature, to read terrain, to find water in dry places. As he rode along thinking about it, Caleb realized that if he had to, he could survive in the wilderness because of all the things that Rab Sinclair had taught him.

And Rab's reward for the patience and instruction was that now Caleb had stolen twelve horses – really, eleven because the horse he was riding was one Rab had given him – and five saddles.

Leading the horses, Caleb was not making great time.

The first blue light of dawn found him nearing Bernal Creek, and he was glad to find a little water flowing.

He dismounted at the creek and gave the horses a chance to get water.

It had all come too fast to do it right.

If they were going to do it right, Caleb should have had the spare horses in place two or three days in advance. As it was, the horses would already have traveled a bit more than sixty miles. His plan was to leave in the middle of the night and get the horses at least to the Pecos livery that day. He'd put them in the livery for the night, and tomorrow he would ride almost to Santa Fe.

Matty Rio and the rest of the outfit would be leaving Rab's ranch about now. They'd ride beyond Bernal Creek and make camp close to where they intended to stop the stagecoach. When the stagecoach came through around noon tomorrow, their horses would be rested and ready to make a fast run to Santa Fe.

"There's no turning back," Caleb said as he got back in the saddle and took the lead ropes. He gave the ropes a bit of a pull to get the horses started.

"If I was going to back out of this thing, I'd have to do it right here," he said. "If I keep going from here, I have to do my part for the outfit."

He hesitated one more moment, and then he gave his horse a little leg and drove the horses through the low water and on to the other side.

- 8 -

Since before the War, Fort Union provided most of the jobs east of the Sangre de Cristo Mountains, both in southeastern Colorado and northeastern New Mexico.

The fort consisted of numerous adobe buildings on four hundred acres of land. The army hired civilians to work its own livestock and let contracts to forage agents for everything from beans to hay. The army had its own cattle herds, but often found that it had to supplement its herds from local sources. In its history, Fort Union had provided provisions to all the forts in the New Mexico District. Though its primary function had always been protecting the Santa Fe Trail and local settlements, the Fort became the center of commerce in area.

The quartermaster's office alone hired anywhere from a hundred to four hundred civilian employees at various times. Civilians got contracts for construction projects at the fort, and it seemed that there was always construction. They got contracts for caring for livestock or providing freight services. In a fort full of cavalrymen and soldiers, some civilians even hired on as watchmen.

But in recent years, it seemed that every time Rab came to the fort more civilians had been discharged than the last time.

The officers quarters and offices, which included the quartermaster's office, were located in a long, adobe building inside the fort. Out front was a large parade ground with a picket fence around it. The building faced to the east so that Rab had a view of the mountains to the west as he rode up to the quartermaster's office.

He'd traded mounts the second day driving the cattle and today was back on the blue roan. The sun was hanging well above the mountains to the west. They'd made good time on the drive without overworking the cattle.

"We've discharged fifteen civilian employees this month," Lieutenant Eddie Matthews was telling Rab. "What are those men to do for a job now?"

"They can go up to Trinidad and look for work, or down to Las Vegas. There's jobs to be had in Santa Fe."

Matthews scoffed. They were alone in the office, Matthews sitting behind a desk and Rab leaning against the wall, happy not to sit down so as to stretch his legs a little.

"I doubt that between them those men have money enough to afford one stagecoach ride to Santa Fe, much less fifteen," Matthews said darkly.

Eddie Matthews had too much heart to be in the army – it was a thing Rab had noticed before. Whether it was the sometimes cruel use the horses were put to, or the vicious ways the cavalry sometimes dealt with what remained of the Comanche out on the Llano Estacado, or the discharged civilian employees, Eddie always seemed to be in a foul mood for the way the army treated someone or something. It was probably why he rode a desk in the quartermaster's office and not a horse in the cavalry.

"And the worst part is, every time I have to discharge a civilian employee, I have to put a soldier on the job. They get extra pay each day, but it's thirteen cents for unskilled labor – and don't even ask me about skilled labor. It's almost impossible to find anyone in the barracks who has the skills we need to replace civilians. Do you think I've got a decent blacksmith or a talented cooper in any one of those barracks? I can tell you I don't."

Eddie liked to complain, and Rab liked to let him. So long as Eddie Matthews felt that he could complain to Rab, there was a better likelihood that Rab would continue to get contracts for beef cattle from the army.

"The whole damn territory depends on us spend money, and every year it seems that the budget is cut more and more," Eddie said.

He shuffled the papers on his desk.

"Fifty cattle?"

"All here," Rab said, pleased that they'd not lost a single steer on the drive north. Though Vazquez and Kuwatee would be pretty poor hands if they couldn't drive fifty cattle thirty miles.

"I'll cut your pay," Lieutenant Matthews said.

Rab took the moment to ask a question he'd been wondering about.

"You got any deserters?"

Lieutenant Matthews laughed his scoffing laugh again.

"Up to my eyeballs in 'em," he said.

"Feller down in Las Vegas. They call him Union Joe. He's wearing a pair of cavalry boots."

Eddie Matthews shrugged.

"I don't know any of their names. Union Joe? Did he fight for the Union in the War?"

"Too young for that," Rab said. "I thought maybe they called him 'Union' for absconding from this place."

"Could be," Eddie Matthews said. "I can find out if we've got a Joe missing, but it might take a while."

"Ain't worth the trouble," Rab said.

Lieutenant Matthews counted from a cash box the money for the cattle and handed it to Rab, who put it into a wallet that he tucked inside his buckskin coat.

"What about a feller goes by the name of Matty Rio?"

Lieutenant Matthews looked up sharply.

"Now that's a name I know," he said. "Younger man, probably in his mid-twenties. Fancy dresser."

"That's right," Rab said.

"He was up in Trinidad for a while," Lieutenant Matthews said. "Thought of himself as a gambler, I guess.

Tried to cheat a couple of soldiers who were on leave. The whole thing turned bad, with a fight and a shooting."

Rab frowned. He didn't think of Matty Rio as being much of a fighter. He thought the man appeared to be all bluff.

"Matty Rio shot a soldier?"

"Hell, no," Lieutenant Matthews said, his tone full of complaint now. "One of our privates was half drunk, and he drew on this Matty Rio character and fired. Missed Rio and shot the bartender."

"Shot the bartender," Rab repeated.

"Creased him. Didn't kill him. A captain and I rode up there and took the two men into custody. The sheriff up in Trinidad turned them over to us. We had a court martial, and I've still got a private in the stockade. The boy who was smart enough not to draw his pistol only stayed in the stockade for a month, but the one who shot the bartender is in for a year."

"What happened to Matty Rio?"

"Matt Rivers," Lieutenant Matthews said. "The sheriff in Trinidad tracked down who he really is. Matt Rivers. He was trying the same card hustling up in Denver before he turned up in Trinidad. With the same results, except that the man who drew on him got shot."

"By Matty Rio – or Rivers?" Rab asked.

"Nope. In Denver he was gambling in a place that had a bouncer in the corner. The bouncer was armed with a Winchester," Lieutenant Matthews said. "He put down the man that Rivers was trying to cheat. The law in Denver told Rivers to get out of town."

Eddie Matthews narrowed his eyes, studying Rab's

face and looking for a reaction to the news. But Rab Sinclair was a hard man to read.

"I'm obliged to you for the information," Rab said.

"You having some trouble with these two? Matt Rivers and Joe?"

Rab shook his head.

"You know that boy Caleb who sometimes works for me?"

"Sure."

"He's taken up with these two and a couple of others."

Lieutenant Matthews frowned.

"I'd get him away from them pretty fast," he said.

"I reckon I will," Rab said.

Lieutenant Matthews twisted his mouth, picking his back teeth with his tongue, and he studied Rab for a moment.

"You don't strike me as a rancher," Matthews said.

"How's that?" Rab asked.

Matthews shrugged.

"I see a mess of ranchers in this job," the lieutenant said. "Most of 'em are wound pretty tight. Always arguing over prices, trying to get a little something more out of the army. Complaining that we cheat 'em. It's always some fight every time a rancher walks through that door. But you're different. I give you a price and you just hold a hand out for your money. Every other rancher, they shout and holler at their hands and cuss about every little thing. I ain't never heard you raise your voice, Rab."

Sinclair smiled and shrugged.

"I reckon maybe I'm different from some others."

"You ever think about a price you'd ask for that place of yours?" Matthews asked.

"Haven't thought much about it," Rab said. "It's a nice little valley where my place is. I'm partial to it."

"Maybe so," Matthews said, squinting at Rab. "But you ain't partial to raising cattle, I reckon."

Rab didn't make any response.

"I've got a brother back east. He ain't in the army. But our family has a little money, and he wrote me a while back saying he was coming out this way to see me and might be interested in an opportunity. If he had your place, I could see to it that he had a buyer for his cattle."

Rab chuckled.

"I reckon you could see to it," Rab said with a grin.

"Anyway. My brother ain't here yet. Next letter I get might say he decided not to come at all. But think about it. If you want to sell, come and see me. Maybe I'll leave the army and raise cattle myself."

As he left the quartermaster's office, Rab gave some thought to whether or not to share with Evangeline what he'd learned about Matty Rio's past. He knew she was concerned about Caleb and what he'd gotten into, and he didn't want to worry her more with rumors.

While Rab was getting his pay from the Lieutenant Matthews, the rest of his outfit were helping to get the herd into the stockyards. Kuwatee and Vazquez rode up on their mounts.

Rab took their pay from his wallet and gave it to

both of them.

"I'll see you boys back in Las Vegas," Rab told them. "Evangeline and I are going to ride out to Rociada."

Kuwatee nodded, having already guessed that they would.

Rociada was just a tiny village above Las Vegas toward the mountains, but Rab enjoyed following the valleys and getting a closer look at the peaks. There was a cantina there where they could get a room for the night, and it was for both of them a favorite place to go for a feast.

Evangeline had already put all they would need on one of the mules, and they decided they would leave out that afternoon, getting part of the way while there was still daylight.

Kuwatee and Vazquez intended to spend the night at the fort and make the ride back to Las Vegas the next day.

- 9 -

Rociada sat in a flat valley, almost completely surrounded by tall foothills of the Sangre de Cristo. To the south, dominating over the lower hills, Hermit's Peak seemed like the bald head of a storybook giant.

The valley was full of good hay and storage barns. There weren't as many cattle as one might expect because the farmers here had found that the army paid well for their hay, but a few herds pastured in the valley. There were series of connected valleys all through here as the fingers of the foothills sloped down and pressed into the flat land, and Rab Sinclair had fallen in love with the mountains and the valleys and the creeks that flowed out of the one and into the other. The area was also heavily forested with pines and some oaks, and Rab had a love for trees that couldn't always be satiated in the dry and sandy lowlands of New Mexico.

Leading their one pack mule and riding his favorite roan, Rab Sinclair was always filled with a special joy when he and Evangeline could slip away into these valleys.

"We should build a little cabin up in the mountains, give up the ranch, and live a hermit life," Rab said.

Evangeline murmured something.

"What's that?" he asked.

"I thought we were living a hermit life," she said.

Some years before, a Jesuit from Italy somehow found his way to New Mexico Territory. He climbed up the bald peak overlooking Las Vegas, found a little cave, and spent about three years living there as a hermit.

Still, Catholic pilgrims came to Las Vegas to visit the cave as if it somehow held some mystical power simply for having been a priest's hideaway. A person could only reach the cave from above, and two or three times a year some Catholic pilgrim would slip on the rocks and fall to a hard landing, breaking a leg or an arm or sometimes a skull. Though he had often listened to his father rage against the practices of papists, Rab was fascinated by the priest and the notion of living as a hermit in the mountains.

"We go into town once or twice a week," Rab said. "Somebody's always stopping by the ranch for a visit. I'd hardly say we're hermits."

"You couldn't last as a hermit," Evangeline said.

"Hermits have to stay put. You don't have a stay-put bone in your body, Rabbie. You've got too much wandering to do."

Rab laughed.

"Do I wander?" he said.

"Where are we right now, and why are we here?"

Rab laughed and gave a slight touch with his heel to Cromwell's side to keep the roan moving along.

"I reckon I do enjoy getting out once in a while."

Riding through the valley, it was hard not to think of the time he'd spent with the Ute People, both as a child and as an adult.

"The Weenuche Ute are among the finest horsemen I've ever known," Rab said. "I rate them equally as competent on the back of a horse as the Comanche."

Evangeline wrinkled her nose and looked at him from the corners of her eyes.

"As good as the Comanche?" she asked.

Though there were still some Ute in the Four Corners area of New Mexico Territory, there were none around Las Vegas so far as Evangeline knew. She had never seen a Ute, at least not knowingly. But she had seen Comanche and knew they were skilled horsemen.

"The Ute use leather stirrups that hang from the horse's mane," Rab told her.

"It gives them a unique ability to control the horse, and it also provides an advantage in combat. With these stirrups, Ute warriors can drop to the side of the horse and shoot from under the belly."

"Can they hit anything while shooting from under

the belly of a horse?"

"I've seen them do it," Rab said. "I even tried it a time or two when I was younger."

"Did you hit anything?"

Rab laughed, giving the reins a slight tug as the roan tried to take a bite from some grass beside the road.

"My recollection is that I usually ended up on the ground with some fresh bruises and a mouthful of dirt. I also found the stirrups, which were short, to be more than a little uncomfortable over distances of just about any length."

Evangeline always enjoyed listening when Rab was feeling talkative. She'd never known anyone like him who had been across so much of the country. She'd been into west Texas a couple of times, and Rab had taken her up into the mountains in Colorado Territory, but other than that the farthest she'd ever gone was from California to Santa Fe, and that had been done in the back of a bumping and jarring stagecoach.

"Chief Ouray told me that the Comanche first acquired horses from the Ute," Rab said. "I don't know if it is true or just bragging, but the similarities in horsemanship between the two tribes make it seem likely enough. I do know that at times the Comanche and the Ute raided white settlements and other Indian villages together, so it could be true."

They rode on a ways together, Rab's talkative mood had vanished, but Evangeline kept watching him. As they rode, his eyes scanned the landscape. Sometimes he would stop and stare for a while.

"Look there," Rab said at one point, nodding off to a point far across the valley.

"Horses," Evangeline said, noting a herd of about thirty or forty wild horses grazing in the valley.

"Look closer," Rab said.

"Antelope," Evangeline laughed, seeing a small pack of antelope grazing near the horses.

"You watch close enough, and you'll see just about anything," Rab said.

A hawk sailed overhead and then dropped like a spear into the wide pasture land. It emerged from the tall grass with some sort small animal dangling from its claws.

"I could sit out here forever and just watch God's creation do its work around us."

Evangeline smiled at him.

"And be a hermit," she said.

"Build a little adobe hut near a creek, maybe at the base of one of these hills. It would be a life," Rab said.

"Until you decided that you'd seen enough of creation in this valley and wanted to move on to the next one," Evangeline said.

"I might do," Rab said. "Maybe we should think about finding a new valley. This one, or another one."

"Are you feeling restless?" Evangeline asked.

"A mite bit," Rab confessed.

"As long as you take me with you, I don't care how restless you feel. But I don't want to be left at the ranch to wait and wonder if you'll ever come back."

Rab nodded thoughtfully.

"I reckon I've gotten accustomed to having you around," he said, and though he dropped a note of teasing in his voice, he knew it was true. "I don't believe I'd think of going if you weren't going to go with me."

"What would we do with the ranch?"

"Sell it to Vazquez," Rab said. "Give it to Caleb. Either one of them should be happy to have it."

Evangeline realized that Rab must have been giving some thought to it already.

"We'll talk about it again," she said.

Soon, Rociada came into view. No more than a collection of adobe huts, log cabins, and a couple of stores and a tavern, the village was mostly occupied by the Bacca family who had been in the area since it was a Spanish Territory, before Mexico won independence and before the territory was taken by the United States. But the Baccas were people who could adapt, and when the United States built the fort on the Santa Fe Trail, the Baccas became very wealthy. The village was near enough to the fort that folks who lived in Rociada frequently went to work as laborers at Fort Union. They also sold hay, timber, beans and even horses to the army.

So the village was remote, but also wealthy.

Jose Emmanuel Torres was a short and round man with a thick black mustache and curly black hair. He ran the tavern in Rociada, and he'd never met a stranger. After Rab and Evangeline had taken their horses and the mule to the livery, they went to the tavern where Jose greeted them both with a wide smile and warm embraces.

"Rabbie Sinclair!" he said, coming from behind the counter that served as his bar and throwing his arms around Rab. "Evangeline! I am so happy to see my friends!"

"Hello, Jose," Rab said. "We'd like a room for the night, and a bottle of mescal for now."

Jose nodded.

"I am happy to give you both," he said. "And a feast. We will have a feast tonight!"

Jose Torres, who had married a woman from the Bacca clan, promised a feast as if it was a rare thing and only being offered in celebration of seeing Rab and Evangeline.

"Senor Torres," Evangeline said with a doubtful grin. "Tell me the truth now, were you going to have a feast whether we showed up or not?"

Jose Torres returned her grin.

"Of course I was," he said.

It did not take long before half the village was crowded into Jose Torres's cantina, and everyone who came through the door had another bowl or tray of food. The mescal flowed plentifully so long as Rab continued to share some of his earnings from Fort Union, and they ate and drank late into the evening. Some of the men from the village brought guitars that they played, and some of the women sang and danced. Evangeline joined them in dancing, and only when he'd had too much mescal did Rab allow her to lure him to his feet to join in.

- 10 -

"Stagecoach is late," Union Joe said, looking at his watch. It was the only watch in the outfit, given to him by his father when he'd left to join the army. He never looked at it without a twinge of guilt.

"Stagecoaches run late," Matty Rio said. "It ain't a problem."

The stage road near Pecos was rocky and treacherous in places, but beyond the relay station at Bernal there were flat spots covered in juniper and cottonwoods.

They'd picked a spot where Eduardo could watch from a high cliff and see the coach coming from more than a mile away and signal to the others when it came into view. The plan was to ride out into the road with guns drawn to stop it. Eduardo would watch from the cliff overlooking the road to be sure there were not other travelers coming near. As they made their escape, Eduardo would ride down and join them.

It was a simple and straightforward plan.

"We'll ride out into the road, guns drawn, and when the coach comes on us, we'll stop it," Matty Rio explained.

Matty Rio had a gun, a pearl-handled Colt Army, and Chavez kept a scattergun. Bud Woolery had a Remington revolver that he used for shooting dogs and cats. But none of the rest of the outfit was armed. So after Caleb Morgan left, Matty and the others broke into Rab Sinclair's cabin. They found six good '66 Winchester repeaters and boxes of ammunition, and they took all of the rifles. They tried their hands at shooting a bit on some wild horses on Sinclair's ranch. Wool managed to shoot down two of the mustangs, but the herd broke and ran before anyone else could shoot one. But Union Joe did shoot four cows.

These were the guns they would use to hold up the stagecoach.

Now the four of them – Matty, Wool, Union Joe, and Chavez, were all sitting their horses waiting for the signal from Eduardo.

"He's waving," Wool said, and his voice cracked in his excitement.

Matty Rio looked up at the cliff and saw that Eduardo had his hat off and was waving it wildly.

"Let's ride," he said, giving his mount a hard kick

with both heels.

The four members of the gang charged forward out of the flats where they'd camped, hidden behind juniper bushes and a cluster of live oaks.

Just as they rode out, the coach came into view.

Matty Rio and Union Joe both fired their rifles into the air, and the driver on the coach dragged hard on the reins to pull his team to a stop. The coach made a terrible racket as the driver tried to bring it to a stop, the chains and traces rattling like hell and the horses and wheels kicking up a cloud of dust that looked like a grass fire.

In the driver's box, the shotgun rider was already bringing up his gun. Wool didn't wait for conversation. He'd already made up his mind. The coach was not at a stop when Wool's Winchester spit out its flame and smoke, and the bullet smashed the shotgun rider square in the chest. The man jerked violently, and the jehu could hear his breathing get rapid and shallow.

"I'm shot good," he said through gritted teeth.

Wool worked the action on the Winchester and shot the man a second time in the chest.

"Hold your damn fire!" the jehu shouted, but Wool was having fun. He worked the action again and now shot the driver. The shot creased his arm, and the driver dropped from the box and started to run. Wool gave his horse a kick and let out a shout of joy. Shooting stagecoach drivers was more fun than cats and dogs.

The shots had come as a surprise to everyone.

Matty Rio's instructions were to not kill anyone if they could help it. They all knew that there was a difference in the way the law would pursue murderers and the way the law would pursue stagecoach robbers. Road agents were a known hazard of travel. Easterners didn't feel like they'd been West if they hadn't been held up on a stagecoach. Matty Rio and his gang would be just a few more in a large stack of wanted circulars for stagecoach robbers. But murder was a different thing, and the law would come after them. And if the law couldn't catch them, some bounty hunter might. Matty had said to them not to wait to shoot if they thought someone was going to try to be a hero, but he hadn't anticipated open murder.

"Dammit Wool!" Matty shouted, but there was no use stopping him now. The driver ran as fast as he could, but before he'd covered any distance, Wool was on top of him, firing a shot into his back.

Matty was frozen in place, but Union Joe moved quickly.

He was off his horse now and opening the door of the coach.

"Nobody do nothing that'll get you killed," Joe warned the passengers, the barrel of his Winchester ominously stuck inside the open door. "Come on out now, keeping your hands up where we can see them."

Five passengers exited the stagecoach, and their fear was evident. Three of the passengers were men, two traveling alone on business from Las Vegas to Santa Fe. The one woman was traveling with the third man, her husband, and their young daughter. The woman and the girl were both crying.

Chavez did not dismount. Getting back on the horse was too much of a struggle for him. So he kept his Winchester directed at the passengers now lining up outside the coach.

Matty Rio dropped from his saddle, still a little stunned at the sudden violence.

The shotgun rider was slumped in the driver's box. The driver was face down on the road behind them.

Wool was riding back toward the stagecoach.

All of them had bandannas pulled up over their mouths and noses to help disguise their identities, but Matty could see from the lines beside his eyes that Wool was grinning over his murders.

Matty held a canvas sack out to Union Joe. Joe took it from him and held it open toward the passengers.

"Fill that bag with all your valuables. Money, rings, watches. Whatever you've got," he said. "We'll search you, and if you hold back, we'll kill you."

The woman started to remove a ring, but Matty shook his head at her.

"Not you, ma'am. We won't steal from a woman," he said.

He'd heard that other stagecoach robbers did not take from women, and he thought it was a decent flair.

While Joe took the wallets and watches from the three men, Matty Rio climbed up onto the coach. He put the handbrake on to keep the horses from spooking and running in the excitement, and then he dug into the front boot where the strongbox should have been. But there was no strongbox.

"It ain't here," he said.

"What ain't there?" Union Joe said.

"The strongbox. It ain't in here."

Eduardo kept his watch while Matty Rio and Wool

went through the entire coach. They flung luggage and trunks all across the road, opening everything and strewing clothes all over the road. Union Joe led the passengers over to some shade under a cottonwood and told them all to sit down.

Joe was worried about Bud Woolery. Like Caleb Morgan, Joe had signed on for this believing they would try to avoid killing anyone. He wasn't nearly as naive as Caleb. Union Joe knew there was some chance they would have to kill the shotgun rider. Some of those men took their jobs too seriously.

But Wool took too much joy in the killing. And Joe didn't think they were much more than an argument away from Wool gunning down the passengers – the woman and the little girl, too.

"Just be quiet and don't rile us," Joe advised the passengers.

One of them, who looked to be in his late twenties or early thirties, and did not give much appearance of being intimidated, squinted hard at Union Joe. He'd noted the boots.

"You a deserter?" he said.

Joe glared at him but did not respond.

"It's okay, son," the man said. "My name's O'Toole. I rode with the cavalry for a while. Fought the Comanche in Texas. I know how it gets sometimes. You sign up to do a thing, but when you start doing it you find out it ain't what you thought it was going to be."

"What are you talking about?" Joe asked. He felt as if the man, O'Toole, had read his mind and was referring to the stagecoach robbery.

"The cavalry," O'Toole said. "I left a mite shy of my enlistment being up, too."

"Hush up," Union Joe breathed at him. "I said not to rile us."

O'Toole noisily sucked at his back teeth.

"Way I see it, it don't matter none whether I rile you or not," O'Toole said. He gave a meaningful glance at the young girl, wrapped in her mother's arms and sobbing. "What's going to happen here is going to happen whether I rile you or not."

Union Joe looked at the woman, the mother, holding her sobbing daughter. The woman's face was stolid, almost defiant. Her husband sat with his arm around his wife's shoulder. The woman wore a light-blue dress, and the girl wore a dark blue skirt and a white blouse. The girl was probably about twelve years old. The woman's face had sharp, drawn lines, and those lines seemed to be getting sharper as she sat there watching Joe.

"Nothing's done yet," Union Joe said.

O'Toole grinned at him.

"I recognize the brands on your horses," he said. "That S-bar brand, that's Rabbie Sinclair's brand."

"So?"

"I know Rab Sinclair ain't involved in what you're doing here, which means those horses is stolen."

O'Toole had worked for Sinclair a number of times, driving cattle and other jobs, and he'd ridden many of Rab's horses.

Union Joe shook the canvas sack he'd tucked into his belt. The passengers' watches and a couple of rings jingled inside the sack.

"They ain't all that's stoled," he said.

O'Toole shrugged his shoulders.

"But we're just passengers on a stagecoach. Stealing from us ain't hardly a thing. But taking from Rabbie Sinclair is like asking to get yourselves shot dead."

Union Joe hissed at him.

"Don't rile us," he said. Now Union Joe took several steps backwards, still keep his gun trained on the passengers, but moving to where he could see the others riffling through the luggage and tearing up the seats on the coach.

O'Toole dropped his voice low.

"Ma'am, I don't mean to alarm you or your daughter, but I think I have to say what I need to say here," he whispered. Though he addressed the mother, he was talking to all of the passengers sitting with him.

"Yes, Mr. O'Toole," the woman said. "Please say what you feel you must."

"I think this is going to come to a violent end. And unless one of you is toting a gun that got past our young cavalryman there, we're at a disadvantage."

The woman's husband tightened his fingers on her shoulder.

"Do you have a suggestion?" he asked.

"The three of us men need to be fast to jump up," O'Toole said. "Get your hands on them, fight for your life. Try to take their guns if you can. The two women need to run for all they're worth. These men will be eager to leave this place, ma'am. If you can run a little ways, it'll be enough. Important thing is that you just keep running. Can you do that?"

"My daughter and I can do that," the woman said, and then she bent her head into her daughter's hair and whispered something that the men could not hear.

"Are you gentlemen prepared to do your manly duty?" O'Toole asked.

The husband, and father, nodded his head. He was a preacher, going to take a church in a village outside of Santa Fe, excited for the opportunity and full of expectation. Though he was not a violent man, he would not shy from violence to protect his family.

"Of course," he said.

The other man also spoke up.

"I'll do what I have to," he said. Of the three, the third man was the youngest and looked the likely sort for a fight. He was well-built and strong. He might have been a farmer or a cowhand, but he was dressed in a fine suit that suggested he was something else. In truth, he was also on his way to Santa Fe, full of expectations. He was a lawyer from Harvard, traveling west to be an aide for the territorial governor. It was an appointment secured for him by his father. The young man was sure it would be the first step on a lucrative career in government. He was hoping he might find himself serving as an ambassador in Europe.

***

"There ain't no strongbox, there ain't no money, and now we're all implicated in two murders for nothing but a sack full of watches," Union Joe said.

Union Joe seethed with anger. They'd all dropped

their bandannas now, and Union Joe spit on the ground between Matty Rio's shined-up boots.

"Who even told you there would be money on this stagecoach?" he asked.

Matty Rio stayed stone-faced and silent. The fact is, he'd overhead a man he knew to be a Las Vegas bank teller talking about a shipment of money to Santa Fe. He got the impression from listening to the conversation that the money shipments were regular. But it appeared now there were not regular shipments of cash from Las Vegas to Santa Fe.

Matty Rio bit his lip, then swallowed hard. Inside, he felt scared. Everything had been planned so perfectly, and in a short space of time it had all gone wrong. But he did not want the others to know he was scared.

Chavez had climbed down off his horse and was now watching the passengers, still sitting on the ground under the cottonwood.

O'Toole felt the old tension he always felt just before action against the Indians. A tightening in his chest, a twisting in his stomach. He was watching the anger on the faces of the men at the stagecoach, and he had a strong feeling about where this was going. The one that killed the shotgun rider and the coach driver, he killed because he liked it. O'Toole could see it in the sneer on his face. The others were just boys, really. Old enough to be involved in this – old enough, certainly, to know better – but not old enough to disguise their fear. The killer would talk them into it, or he would just start killing the passengers. And among the others, there was not a man who would stand up to them.

"It's going to be soon, now," O'Toole said. "Everyone be ready to do your part."

The husband set his teeth.

The lawyer adjusted his legs so that he could spring up from the ground in a hurry. The mother whispered into her daughter's hair.

"They're going to decide they've got to get out of here, and someone's going to ask what about us. That's when it'll come."

O'Toole was a steady hand. He was on his way to Santa Fe to see about becoming a cattle investigator, intending to make a living hanging rustlers. He wasn't afraid of action. But he did not like being at a disadvantage.

"We should get going before someone comes along," Matty Rio said. Then he glanced at the passengers under the cottonwood tree.

"Wool, you unhook the team from the coach and we'll lead the team off a couple of miles."

"Hell on that," Wool said, and he took a step toward the passengers.

"Here it comes," O'Toole said.

Wool walked several steps toward them, and without warning he raise up the Winchester rifle.

"Now!" O'Toole shouted as he sprang up from the ground.

O'Toole had picked Wool as the most dangerous of them, and figured that should be the one he'd take on. So the former cavalryman charged forward toward the one in the worn buckskin coat.

The Winchester erupted, the blast echoing like thunder in the valley. The shot caught O'Toole in the stomach and felt like he'd been kicked by a horse. But O'Toole pressed on, reaching out to grab hold of the rifle barrel and swinging a wild punch into Wool's jaw.

The husband went for Chavez, the one nearest to them. Chavez panicked and started to run.

The woman and her daughter were quick to their feet, but they were not as fast as the lawyer. He took off down the road, back toward Bernal, running as fast and as hard as he could, followed by the mother and daughter.

Matty Rio didn't know what to do other than to play his part. He leveled his Winchester and shot down the man who was chasing after Chavez.

O'Toole kept a hand on the rifle barrel and threw another punch at Wool, connecting this time with the side of his head. The punches were hard, and Wool was stunned, but the man was leaking blood from his gut and had to be losing strength. Wool jerked the Winchester loose and clubbed the man with the butt of the gun.

O'Toole went down hard, and Wool cocked the Winchester and fired another shot into O'Toole's gut.

"That should do for you," Wool laughed.

He quickly assessed the situation.

The mother could have run faster, but she was running behind her daughter – both encouraging and shielding the girl. Wool cocked the lever on the Winchester and took a good sight down the barrel. When he had the mother's back lined up, he pulled the trigger.

The shot knocked the woman violently from her feet, and the woman somersaulted to the ground, a large red stain rapidly appearing on the back of her dress. The girl stopped and ran to her mother, sobbing violently.

Wool leapt into his saddle, and drawing up his reins he gave the horse leg and galloped toward the girl. The lawyer was running hard and leaving the girl and her mother behind.

Holding the Winchester in one hand and riding so close to the girl that he could have touched her, Wool pointed the barrel at the girl. As he got up even with her, he pressed the barrel against her back just between her shoulder blades and he pulled the trigger. She convulsed violently as she fell on top of her mother.

Matty Rio thought he was going to be sick.

Chavez could not watch.

Union Joe, though, he watched the whole thing with only one thought in his mind: The army was never this bad.

Wool never stopped.

He rode right on past the girl, even as she collapsed, and darted past the lawyer.

His horse skidded to a stop as Wool drew up and then wheeled the animal back toward the lawyer.

The lawyer turned and started running again, but he was exhausted and stumbled. He got back to his feet, his mouth full of dust and his heart racing. He knew he was running back toward the stagecoach and the others, but the man on the horse was terrifying.

He could hear the horse galloping fast behind him, and then felt a tremendous crack on the back of his skull.

Wool wielded the Winchester as a club, swinging it so that the barrel smashed the lawyer in the back of the head.

Now Wool wheeled around again, riding back up to the lawyer and drawing the reins. He sat his horse, grinning down at the lawyer as he struggled to get to his feet. His head was spinning and he was having trouble remembering anything or thinking about anything.

"I believe I split your skull," Wool laughed. "Hell, boys, I think I see his brains."

Wool worked the lever on the Winchester and pointed it down at the lawyer's head.

"Can I get a bullet through the hole I've already made?" he asked with a grin.

The Winchester echoed again and the lawyer slumped to the ground, his head turned into a red and pink mush.

"I believe I can," Wool said, full of pride.

He looked up at the others.

Matty Rio looked aghast. Chavez was dragging his horse over to the stagecoach so that he could step up onto the coach to then get into the saddle. Union Joe was just watching.

"Now we don't have to worry about the team of horses," he said. "We can just go on."

And that's what they did.

- 11 -

Rab Sinclair and Evangeline came out of the mountains around Rociada on a trail that wasn't much more than a deer path and then took the road south toward Las Vegas.

"There's a reason I don't over-indulge in liquor very often," he said, his head pounding with every step that Cromwell took.

Evangeline laughed, but she didn't feel much better, herself.

"We should go visit Senor Torres more often," she

said. "I seldom have more fun."

On the ranch, Evangeline was just another cowhand. She'd taken to wearing dirty old trousers and buckskin leggings years ago. From a distance, she and Rab looked more like twin brothers than man and woman. During the festivities at Senor Torres's cantina, she'd been persuaded to put on one of the colorful dresses the other women wore. She'd danced and mimicked their way of flinging the dresses around in a way that exposed her long, creamy legs, and Rab had found the whole thing so enticing that he'd bought her the dress for twenty dollars.

"I don't reckon I can afford too many visits. I ain't never been so under the mescal that I spent twenty dollars on a dress," he said. "My Lord, I hope you didn't forget to pack it."

Evangeline grinned at him.

"You were quite taken," she said.

"You were quite fetching," he replied. "I reckon sometimes I'm guilty of forgetting just how long your legs are."

Rab reined in the roan and slipped his canteen off the saddle horn. He took a big drink and held the canteen out for Evangeline. She also took a big drink.

"Next time, we'll stay an extra day to recover," Evangeline said.

"I don't know that I could survive a next time. Or that I would want to."

Evangeline took another drink from the canteen. The water was fresh from a spring and still very cool. It felt good in her throat. Rab pushed the cork back into the top and slung it back over the pommel. As he did, he caught sight of someone down on the road riding up toward them.

Even from a distance, Rab recognized the man. Most folks had a manner in the way they sat a horse, or in the way they wore a hat. Vazquez had a habit of putting too much pressure into his stirrups so that his legs always seemed stiff, even when the horse was just at a walk.

"Why would Vazquez be all the way up here?" Rab said.

Evangeline leaned forward on her horse, peering at the rider. Rab's eyesight was a bit better than hers.

"Is it Vazquez?" she asked.

"Looks to be," he said.

They walked their horses a bit father to meet Vazquez who reined in when he got up to them.

"I thought it was you," Vazquez said. His face showed he was burdened and this was no friendly greeting or coincidental encounter. "I wasn't for sure you'd gone to Rociada, but I thought it was a good bet. Anyway, I'm glad I found you."

"You're looking for us?" Rab asked, and in a moment his hangover was gone. Rab felt himself getting alert Vazquez would have never come looking for him if there wasn't trouble.

Vazquez leaned forward, rubbing his horse's neck.

"No easy way to tell you this, Rab," Vazquez said. "When Kuwatee and I got back to your place, there'd been some trouble. Looks like someone stole some of your rifles, and Kuwatee says you've got a dozen horses missing."

"Is Caleb all right?" Evangeline asked.

Vazquez twisted his mouth.

"We didn't find Caleb at the place," Vazquez said. "But there's more. Someone shot some of your cattle – I think it was four head – and a couple of those mustangs that run your ranch."

Rab sat his saddle like a statue. Evangeline, though, could tell he was seething with anger.

"We reckon it must have happened two days ago."

"What else?" Rab said.

"Yesterday, around noon, the stagecoach from Las Vegas to Santa Fe was stopped a few miles beyond the Bernal relay station. When the coach didn't show up at Pecos after a while, they sent a couple of riders to find it. When the riders found it, they found a slaughter. All the passengers were shot. Your friend O'Toole, the one who rode with us to get that herd from Texas that time?"

"Yeah?"

"He was one of the passengers on the stage," Vazquez said. "All the others were dead. Executed. But O'Toole was shot twice in the gut, and he was still alive when they found him. They put him on the stagecoach and drove it back to the Bernal station, and then they sent riders up to get Sheriff Romero."

"Is O'Toole still alive?"

Vazquez shook his head.

"I don't know, Rab. If he is still alive, he won't be long. They kept him at the relay station in Bernal. He's shot up pretty bad – gut shot twice. You know what that means. A doctor went with Sheriff Romero, and his opinion was that O'Toole should stay put. So the last I knew, he was still there and still alive, but he's not going to survive."

Rab nodded. A gut shot was like as not a mortal wound, and it was no easy way to go. If O'Toole was still hanging on a day later, he was doing better than most. Although Rab had known men who had their insides torn to shreds by bullets but hung on for four or five days.

"I'm not telling you things you haven't guessed at Rab, but O'Toole was conscious the whole time, and when Sheriff Romero got there, he was able to give a statement about what happened. Said it was five men who did it. One did all the shooting, but there were four who stopped the stagecoach and another who kept a watch. He also said the four horses he saw all had the S-bar brand on them."

Rab glanced over at Evangeline. He could see from the look on her face that she was thinking the same thing that he was thinking.

"Caleb?" Evangeline said.

"He wasn't with them," Vazquez said. "O'Toole gave descriptions, and Caleb wasn't one of them."

Rab nodded. The horses used in the stagecoach robbery were the ones stolen from his ranch.

"Four plus a lookout," Rab said. "That accounts for five of my horses, but Kuwatee said a dozen were missing. Sounds like they took twelve so they would have fresh horses waiting."

"That's the sheriff's thinking on it," Vazquez said.

"And someone had to be with those horses, somewhere along the trail," Rab said.

"Caleb," Evangeline said, and this time it was not a question.

"The descriptions O'Toole gave were pretty good," Vazquez said. "They wore bandannas initially, but dropped those. But a man wearing fancy clothes with a pearl-handled revolver in a red sash. Another in a worn buckskin coat with holes in it. Another with cavalry boots. And a fat Mexican."

Rab nodded. Vazquez didn't need to say any more.

"I've got warrants for horse theft, stagecoach robbery and murder," Vazquez said. "Named on them are Matty Rio, Bud Woolery, a man known only as Union Joe, and that boy from town Chavez. I've got a couple of other warrants, too. We figure Eduardo was the lookout. O'Toole never got a good look at him. Also, I've got a warrant for horse theft for Caleb Morgan."

Rab took his pipe and tobacco pouch from his pocket and glanced at Evangeline while he filled the pipe. Tears welled in her eyes. As much as Rab said that Caleb should be on his own, Evangeline had developed a fondness for him and treated him – if not like a son, then like a little brother. Rab struck a match and puffed the pipe to get the tobacco lit.

"Well, hell, Vazquez," Rab said, a real look of disgust on his face. "When I saw you on the road, I knew you weren't toting good news. So what's next with these warrants?"

"The sheriff wants me to bring them in," Vazquez said. "I'm about to get started looking for them. It could be that the warrant for Caleb should have someone else's name on it. We don't know for sure that he was involved."

Rab sighed heavily.

"You say they shot a couple of those mustangs on my ranch?"

"Looks that way, Rab. O'Toole said they were all toting Winchesters and he was the one who said they looked like your guns. What we're thinking is they stole the guns and horses and then did a little practice shooting on your livestock."

"Damn, that makes me mad," Rab said. "Hard to believe Caleb was involved in that."

"Like I said, we can't say for certain he was," Vazquez said.

"Maybe," Rab said. "But we're not children, here, Vazquez. We know what happened, and wishing it was different don't make it so. I reckon if you're going after him, I'm going with you."

Vazquez nodded.

"I figured you would."

- 12 -

Caleb Morgan still did not know exactly what had gone wrong, but he knew it was something.

The others all rode ahead of him, and Caleb was in the back pushing the spare mounts. The plan, originally, was to leave the horses at a livery somewhere around Santa Fe so that Rab Sinclair would be able to reclaim them. But when the rest of the outfit changed horses to fresh mounts, Matty Rio told Caleb to bring the horses they'd been riding.

"We're going to need them, after all," Matty said.

They skirted Santa Fe, avoiding the city and trying not to be seen, a difficult challenge in a city where a man standing on a high hill at the north could see all the way across to a man standing on a high hill to the south. Without question, people in the city had seen them ride the Fort Union Road as it curled past the southern tip of the Sangre de Cristo Mountains. The road was easily visible from the city, and six mounted men pushing along six spare mounts would certainly draw notice.

This was something that worried Matty Rio.

Had there been money enough, the outfit would have made it to Albuquerque and been able to board separate stagecoaches. By the time news reached Santa Fe from Las Vegas, even if it came by telegraph as it likely would, Matty Rio and his outfit would have been well on their way to Albuquerque.

But with no money, they had no place to go, no place to escape to.

Near dark they camped off the road not far southwest of Santa Fe.

"What happened with the stagecoach?" Caleb asked Matty as they collected what dead wood they could find for a campfire.

He'd left the question unasked ever since the outfit joined him and switched mounts. He could see things went wrong from the way they acted. All Matty Rio said to him was that they were taking all the horses. So Caleb let the others ride ahead and pushed the exhausted horses on ahead of him. He didn't bother tethering them, they were all so worn that none would run. Matty Rio set an easier pace once they were beyond the relay station at Pecos.

"There weren't no strongbox on the stagecoach,"

Matty Rio said. "That's what happened with the stagecoach."

"No strongbox?" Caleb asked. "I thought it was supposed to be full of bank money."

"So we all thought," Matty Rio said, dumping a load of sticks on the ground.

All they had was dead juniper branches, none of them any bigger around than a forearm. Juniper would splutter and pop and make for a lousy fire to try to cook on, and right now that aggravated Matty Rio just as bad as everything else was aggravating him, including Caleb Morgan and his questions.

"So how are we going to get to California?" Caleb asked.

Matty squatted down and started breaking off small pieces of wood to use as kindling.

"Go and get some more wood," he said. "I'm going to start the fire."

Caleb kept looking for more firewood like he was told to, but he had a concern now that the outfit wasn't on its way to California. It was pointless work, gathering firewood for a campfire. The fire wouldn't serve to keep them warm, and the night promised to be chilly. None of them had anything more than a blanket to sleep on. And they had no food to cook on the fire. All the food they had was some jerky wrapped in cheesecloth that Caleb had put in his saddlebag and a can of peaches that Eduardo had brought along. They were in for a hungry, cold night, and now it didn't seem they were even going to make it to California.

Later, when the sun was down and they were all sitting around the fire, Bud Woolery added to Caleb's concerns.

"I don't mind killing a woman," Wool said.

There'd been no conversation. The statement just emerged from him, and Caleb found it both bizarre and frightening.

"You showed no signs of minding it," Union Joe said. "You ever do anything like that in front of me again, and you'd best be ready for me to shoot you."

Wool looked up sharp, but he was grinning at Union Joe.

"I ain't making a joke," Joe said. "That's the worst thing I ever seen a person do, and you're lucky I didn't shoot you down when you done it."

Wool kept on grinning.

"You could try it if you think you can do it," Wool said. "But you might not like the way it comes out."

"What are you talking about?" Caleb Morgan asked.

Matty Rio kicked a stick hanging out of the fire so that sparks jumped up.

"Just don't nobody say nothing else about it," Matty said. "We had trouble when we stopped the stagecoach. Wool shot a couple of people."

"A couple?" Union Joe scoffed. "He murdered the driver and the shotgun rider and five passengers."

"I said don't say no more about it," Matty Rio said.

"And one of the passengers was a little girl and the other one was her mama."

"Killed them?" Caleb asked. He turned toward Matty Rio. "You said nobody was going to get hurt."

"He also said there'd be a strongbox with twenty thousand dollars in it," Union Joe pointed out. "This one is a maniac, and this one is a fool."

"Don't call me a fool," Matty Rio said.

Wool didn't bother saying anything. He'd heard enough and wasn't going to be insulted. No one saw the Remington six-shooter come out of the holster until the hammer was cocked and the trigger squeezed.

Everyone jumped, except Union Joe who fell backwards from the rock he was sitting on.

Caleb jumped up from his rock and stepped over to Joe.

"He's dead," Caleb said. "You shot him right in the face."

Matty Rio held his hands up toward Wool.

"Dammit, Wool, put that thing away. You can't go killing the men in our outfit."

"He shouldn't have called me a maniac," Wool said.

"If you don't want to be called a maniac, stop acting like one," Matty said.

Caleb thought Matty Rio sounded scared, and he realized they should all be scared. This whole thing had gone terribly wrong, and Caleb knew for sure they would be wanted for those murders back at the stagecoach. And now Union Joe was shot dead by one of their own.

Union Joe took a bullet for what he said about Wool, but Matty had a way of cowing Bud Woolery. At least, he thought he did.

"Holster that gun and drag that body away from our camp," Matty Rio said. "I ain't sleeping in no camp with a dead man."

The tension in the camp was thicker than the smoke hanging in the air from the fire. No one moved or said a word. For a moment, Caleb was certain that Wool was going to do for Matty Rio in the same way he'd done for Union Joe, but then Wool started to laugh. He stood up and holstered his gun.

"Yeah," Wool said, his grinning face lit by the flames from the fire. "I don't want to sleep in a camp with no dead body, neither."

***

Rab Sinclair had known some tomboys in his life. He'd known one who'd been a hard-drinking woman who wore pants, chewed tobacco, and skinned mules for a Santa Fe freighter to earn her living. He'd known another who was raised up in the mountains by an old trapper. The man's son and daughter had become trappers, too. That had been years back, when his own father was still alive and Rab was just a boy. Back then, that old trapper and his family lived so far removed from anyone else that the girl hadn't really been a tomboy so much as she just didn't know any other way.

It occurred to him that Evangeline was a bit of a tomboy herself. She liked some girly things. She had an old silver-handled hairbrush, and a mirror matching with a matching silver handle, and most evenings she'd sit and brush her long hair for the longest time. She liked to be clean, too. Evangeline would bathe regularly. Even out on the trail, she'd find a creek and wash herself.

But watching her now, Rab couldn't help but notice

the way she was similar to some of the other tomboys he'd known.

She wore a beat-up old hat, hide colored but stained with dust and sweat. She wore britches covered over with buckskin leggings and a buckskin coat almost the same as Rab's. The clothes were tools, like anything else. She'd look ridiculous punching cows in one of them colorful Mexican dresses like she wore at Senor Jose Torres's cantina.

But those other tomboys Rab had known, none of them could have worn the colorful dress and done it as much credit. That was the difference between Evangeline and those others he'd known. They were all good enough to drive a mule team or trap a beaver, but a man wouldn't have wanted to see them when they started to remove layers in favor of something prettier to wear.

They were standing in the yard at the relay station in Pecos, giving their mounts a rest. Vazquez was inside, talking to the station manager.

"What are you looking at?" Evangeline said, casting a sideways glance at Rab.

"Just looking at you," Rab said.

"What for?"

Rab swept the scenery with his eyes.

The station sat within sight of the Pecos River, running strong in its green, cottonwood-lined banks as it came down out of the mountains. To the east, they could see Starvation Peak, standing tall over other mesas that formed the last of the Sangre de Cristo mountains. To the west was the tall Glorieta Mesa. Beyond the stagecoach station, to the north, were the tall peaks and pine forests of the mountain range. It was, objectively, a gorgeous view of God's craft.

"I reckon you're the prettiest thing around here to look at," Rab said.

Evangeline blushed and shook her head, smiling in spite of herself.

"Hush," she said.

"You know this could turn out poor," Rab said. "We don't know what Caleb's part in this might be. But it's horse theft and murder for the rest of them. The only reason Vazquez ain't got a murder warrant on Caleb is because O'Toole didn't identify him as being with them."

Evangeline nodded.

"I know what we're doing," she said.

"You could turn back," Rab said. "Go back to the cabin."

Evangeline frowned.

"I have to be a part of this, Rab," she said. "I feel a responsibility toward Caleb. We've had him with us for some time."

Rab nodded. He felt the same responsibility, maybe more sharply than Evangeline did.

After meeting Vazquez on the road from Rociada, Rab and Evangeline rode back to their ranch with the deputy sheriff. They did not waste time there. Though the cabin was in disarray, they only gathered what they needed for an extended journey. Rab confirmed twelve missing horses and the missing guns. They got two fresh pack mules and packed panniers on both of them. They also got two fresh mounts.

They brought the blue roan and the buckskin so that

they would have spare mounts. Neither horse was over-fatigued from the cattle drive. Rab loaned a spare horse to Vazquez, also.

From the ranch they went to the stagecoach relay station at Bernal and learned that O'Toole had succumbed to his wounds. O'Toole was a former cavalryman who left the army short of his enlistment term, but Rab Sinclair had found him to be dependable whenever he hired O'Toole for cattle drives and other work around the ranch. Rab never questioned him about why he left the army. The Comanche and the Apache both were cruel enemies who could drive a man to the very edge of what he could endure. When they fell upon an enemy, their brutality was horrifying. The cavalry at times was hardly any better. The two sides traded cruelties back and forth so that it was no wonder, to Rab, when a man from either side came to a point where he could take no more. From what Rab knew of the man, he doubted that O'Toole's failing was courage.

The men at the Bernal station shared what they could of O'Toole's story.

The descriptions he provided left no doubt for Rab that the gang that held up the stagecoach was Matty Rio's bunch. It was also evident that only one of them did the killing.

"That's going to be the one they call 'Wool,'" Rab told Vazquez.

After leaving the Bernal station, they rode out a ways until they came to the place where the hold up and murders had taken place.

"This is it here," Vazquez said when they came up to the place. "I rode out here with Sheriff Romero after we spoke to O'Toole at the Bernal relay station."

Rab Sinclair could read tracks like an Indian scout.

Rab dismounted and looked over the place. Someone with the stagecoach company had already come along and gotten the coach, and the tracks were muddled with all the riders who'd been through in the two days since the robbery. But even so, Rab was able to find the tracks of some of his stolen horses. Seeing them was important to him. He could spot the tracks of the big draft horse, and even in the hard-packed sand of the roadway, he could see where the draft horse stood without its heavy burden, and distinguish those tracks from the ones where Chavez was on top of the horse.

He also satisfied himself that Caleb Morgan had not been at the scene of the robbery and murder.

Once Rab had seen what he wanted to see, they continued on to the relay station at Pecos where they were now. Along the way, Rab had picked out from the saddle the tracks from his horses on the road. Being able to find the tracks from the saddle meant they could pursue quickly.

At last, Vazquez came out of the Pecos relay station, and he walked to where Rab and Evangeline stood waiting for him. The sun was getting low and they would not be able to ride in daylight much longer, but there had been no discussion yet about pushing on or making camp.

"The station manager saw a boy about twenty years old come through here the day before the stagecoach robbery," Vazquez said. "He was leading six horses. He wasn't in a hurry. He didn't stop to make conversation, which is uncommon enough. He took note of the brand on the horses."

"S-bar?" Rab said, already certain of the answer.

"That's the one," Vazquez said.

"How much money did they get in the robbery?" Rab asked.

"Just what they took off the passengers," Vazquez said. "Obviously, we don't know for sure how much that was. But O'Toole said he thought it was less than a hundred dollars in cash, and a couple of watches."

"Doesn't make sense to kill all those folks for a little bit of money like that," Rab said.

"O'Toole, before he died, said they were looking for a strongbox," Vazquez said. "He said the one we figure to be Matty Rio got pretty agitated when he couldn't find it. Sheriff Romero thinks they were under the impression that there would be a strongbox on the stagecoach."

As he considered it, Rab talked it out with Vazquez.

"So they didn't get a lot of money," he said. "And we know they didn't start out with much money. They're not going to get very far. My guess is that we'll find them in a Santa Fe saloon still trying to concoct a plan to hold up a bank or another stagecoach."

"I just don't understand why Caleb would do it," Evangeline said.

"He's been led in a wrong direction," Rab said. "He joined up with this outfit of ruffians, looking to become a man, and they've led him off in a bad way."

Vazquez kicked dirt with his toe and glanced to the west.

"It's getting late, Rab," he said. "We won't make Santa Fe before dark. The station manager said we're welcome here for the night. What's your thought? Do we push on a little farther or bed down here? He's got a few bunks in a room in the back."

Rab turned his nose up at the relay station – a squat, adobe building with open holes for windows. His preference was to push on. The truth was, Rab would have pushed on through the night if he was alone. Matty Rio and his outfit had a large lead on the two-man and one-woman posse. But he also knew that it could be a while before they had another chance to get a bed that wasn't on the ground and a meal that came off a stove.

"How's the food here?" he asked.

"I've et here a time or two," Vazquez said. "I've had worse."

Rab nodded.

"Might as well stay here for the night," Rab said. "Decent beds, somebody else's cooking. We'll rise early and get a good start. One thing I know for sure about a group like this one that Caleb is running with is that they don't rise early."

- 13 -

Caleb woke feeling cold and hungry.

The others were slow to get from their blankets, and Caleb saw no point in being the first one up and moving around. Careful not to let anyone see, he reached from under his blanket and found the jerky inside his saddlebag lying near him on the ground. He broke off a piece and put it in his mouth. It was salty and a little sweet, and he chewed on it as long as he could make it last.

"What are we going to do?" Chavez asked from under his blanket. Caleb didn't think anyone was awake, but Matty Rio stirred.

"We're going to figure out something," Matty said. "They've got banks in Santa Fe. All this started with us planning to get bank money. Maybe we ride back into Santa Fe and just get the money straight from the bank."

"They'll be looking for us in Santa Fe by now," Caleb said.

"Then we'll ride on to Albuquerque. They got banks, too," Matty Rio said.

"I want to know what we're going to do about food," Chavez said. "A can of peaches ain't gonna cut it."

Matty sat up. The morning was chilly, and on the flats west of Santa Fe there wasn't enough terrain or vegetation to beat down the wind any. He was far more miserable than he thought he was going to be when they entered into this enterprise.

"We've got the cash we took off the stagecoach passengers," Matty said. "We can use that to get some provisions. Then we can start for Albuquerque. When we get there, we'll find something to get into."

Caleb shook his head.

"They'll be looking for us in Santa Fe by now," he said again. "The sheriff in Las Vegas has telegraphed ahead to Santa Fe by now."

Matty Rio nodded.

"They won't be looking for you," he said. "You ride on back into Santa Fe. Get us some beans and some bacon and maybe a bottle or two of whiskey. Then you come back and we'll eat. Then we'll get started for Albuquerque."

Caleb looked back to the east. He couldn't see the town, but he could see the mountain range that marked the location of the town. Santa Fe sat to the west at the base of the Sangre de Cristo Mountains, almost on a line across the mountains from Las Vegas, at least that's how Caleb always imagined it. The road from Las Vegas to Santa Fe made a big curve around the southern tip of the mountain range.

"It'll take me a while to get there, buy provisions, and get back," Caleb said. "Might be four or five hours. We won't get very far along the way to Albuquerque today."

"It don't matter," Chavez said angrily. "Get to town, get some food, and get back here."

Caleb stretched one more time and then pulled the blanket down off of him. He stood up and caught the full force of the chilly morning wind and shivered.

He picked one of the horses and got it saddled and ready to go. Matty Rio gave him some of the cash from the robbery.

"You get back here as quick as you can," Matty said. "Keep your ears open in case they're talking about us back in town."

"Okay," Caleb said.

"Do your best to make sure folks don't take notice of you," Matty said. "Keep your head down and don't talk to anyone more than you have to. You're just there to buy beans and bacon and a bottle or two."

Caleb nodded.

"I'll be all right," he said.

He took up the reins and stepped into the saddle, then drew the horse around to head back toward Santa Fe.

Caleb didn't push the horse overly hard. He went along at a nice, easy walk, glad to be away from the others.

None of this had turned out how he thought it was going to, and he was now wondering what had compelled him to even get involved in this.

There were a few low hills scattered around, and when he was near to one, Caleb rode up the slope a little ways to try to get a look around so that he had his bearings good for when he returned later in the day.

If he returned.

Already it was in Caleb's mind that he might get to Santa Fe and just ride back to the ranch in Las Vegas. The only thing was the horses. Matty Rio and the others still had Rab's horses, and Caleb couldn't just leave the horses and go back. If he was going to go back, he'd have to figure out a way to take the horses with him.

***

Near the long adobe building that housed the headquarters for the district of New Mexico – the territorial government – and just off the Santa Fe plaza, the city was busy growing. The white or mud-colored adobe buildings so common through the city were giving way to larger, stone structures adorned with timber. The city was quickly replacing its historic Spanish charm in favor of buildings that supported the demands of its new Anglo masters. They'd talked of statehood for twenty years already, and a state capitol made of gray stone to reflect its federal virtue was even now under construction.

"Every time I come here, they're putting up another building," Rab said to Vazquez.

"Where are we going?" Vazquez asked as the trio

walked their horses along Palace Road not far from the district headquarters.

"Well, Matty Rio ain't going to be at the Sisters of Loretto chapel, is he?" Rab said. "But if they've stopped in Santa Fe, I might know where to find him."

Down on Bridge Street they turned toward the river until they came to a wide alley running parallel to the river, and there Rab turned into the alley where they found themselves in front of a row of small adobe huts. In the middle of the block, Rab reined in the blue roan and dropped down out of the saddle.

"Wait for me out here," Rab said. "Leave your hand on your pistol, just in case you need to draw it fast."

He handed the reins of the roan to Evangeline and then walked into one of the small adobe huts.

Vazquez couldn't be sure if it was a home or a business. Near the river, the old town got seedier and the folks on the street looked rougher. Every face he saw on the street was bearded and angry looking, almost all of them were rough looking Hispanics or rougher looking white men. Everyone wore guns and long fighting knives on their belts, and everywhere Vazquez looked he was greeted with angry eyes staring back at him. Rab's parting words made Vazquez doubly nervous about sitting in the street with a pretty white woman. Evangeline, though, seemed relaxed, but Vazquez noted her hand was on the grip of the six-shooter hanging in her saddle holster.

"What is this place?" Vazquez asked.

"That's Doogan Vargas's saloon," Evangeline said.

"Oh," Vazquez said.

The son of a Mexican bandit and an Irish whore,

Doogan Vargas was well-known in northern New Mexico Territory as one of the toughest banditos around. It was said that no stagecoach passed unmolested along on the Fort Union Road unless Doogan Vargas decided it could.

"Rab knows Doogan Vargas?" Vazquez asked, sliding his Colt just a touch out of his holster so that it would be easier to draw quickly.

Evangeline laughed playfully.

"Rab knows everyone, Vazquez," she said. "You know that."

The huts were all so close that the windows of one were so near the wall of the next that almost the only light inside the small hut came from the open door. A tiny bar stood at the back of the hut and there were a couple of tables inside, along with some chairs scattered about. Red and green chili peppers hung all over in tightly bound bunches.

The chairs were mostly vacant, though in a back corner, actually behind the bar, three men were sitting at a table, all of them turned to watch the door. The man in the middle started to laugh and loud, booming laugh.

"Rabbie Sinclair!" a shout came from the laughing man.

Doogan Vargas stood up from his chair, his entire appearance absurd. He wore a dull-colored poncho and loose fitting britches, a gunbelt cinched tight over the britches and a gun on each hip. His beard was thick and ginger colored and seemed out of place against his dark complexion. The top of his head was bald, or balding, but from the back he had long, ginger curls that fell to his shoulders.

"Hello, Doogan," Rab said. "Mind if I have a seat?"

"Get him a glass," Doogan said to one of the men sitting at the table with him, and the man moved quickly to get Rab a glass. He poured from the bottle of mescal already on the table.

Rab took a seat across from Doogan, his back to the door.

Doogan, back in his seat now, turned to the men on either side of him.

"This is Rabbie Sinclair," Doogan said. "We shot it out one time on the Cimarron Trail when Rabbie was guarding a freight train. You remember that, Rabbie?"

"I remember," Rab said, his stoic features in sharp contrast to Doogan Vargas's smiling face.

"We ran out of bullets before either one of us killed the other, and we've been friends ever since. Ain't that right, Rabbie?"

"Right, enough," Rab said, a small grin creeping onto his face.

Doogan had no hint of Mexican accent to his voice, having been raised by his Irish mother. The men on either side of him both looked like they had Mexican heritage, though they could have also had some Apache or Comanche heritage. Rab knew that most of the men who rode with Doogan Vargas came from Mexican families who lived in New Mexico or Colorado territories when it was still part of Mexico. Most of them grew up poor, and working for Vargas afforded them opportunities to live a slightly better life.

Vargas started his empire as a bandit, striking wagon trains bound for Fort Union on the Cimarron cutoff. And then he had so many wagons and so much freight that he got into the freighting business, taking stolen supplies to Mexico.

And because Doogan Vargas ran most of the outfits of highwaymen, there was no one to steal from his freight trains.

As the Comanche and Apache in the area were brought under control, the army turned its attention toward highwaymen, and that's when Doogan Vargas decided to go straight – or as straight as he could. His stolen freight wagons, which for years had moved stolen merchandise, now took whiskey distilled from the Santa Fe River all across the territory. And no one bothered Doogan Vargas's wagons.

"I didn't have anything to do with the stagecoach on the Fort Union Road," Vargas said, his smile dropping.

"I didn't think you did," Rab said.

"I reckoned that's why you're here. They say your friend O'Toole was on the coach."

"He was," Rab said.

"Dead now?"

"He is."

Doogan Vargas nodded sadly.

"It is the way of things," he said. "We live in rough country, and we are all rough men."

"Six men with twelve horses came through here in the last two days," Rab said.

"They are the banditos who hit that stagecoach?" Doogan asked.

"They are."

"One of my men saw them, three days ago," he said.

"They came down off the Fort Union Road but never came into the city. They rode off to the southwest. They're camping somewhere out there, though. One of them came into town for supplies day before yesterday."

"What supplies?" Rab asked.

"Food. Beans and bacon."

"They're southwest of the city?" Rab asked.

"They camped there two days ago. I know that much. If they broke camp and left yesterday or today, that's more than I know."

"You couldn't point me to the campsite, could you?" Rab asked.

"Where did you see that boy riding in from yesterday?" Doogan Vargas asked the man to his left.

Unlike Vargas, this man had a heavy accent.

"He come in following the river," the man said. "Along the south bank."

Rab smiled appreciatively.

"Is there anything that happens here that you don't know?" he asked.

Doogan Vargas smiled proudly.

"No."

- 14 -

There was still plenty of daylight when Rab emerged from the small cantina.

Vazquez let out a breath. Neither he nor Evangeline had dropped from their saddles while Rab was inside.

"We'll follow the river out of town," Rab said.

"Doogan Vargas in there?" Vazquez asked.

"He is."

"And he knows where Matty Rio and the others are?"

"He gave us a good place to start."

The fact was, Rab had lost the tracks for the horses. As they neared Santa Fe, the constant traffic on the road had obliterated any specific tracks. And that's what prompted him to ride down to see Doogan Vargas. He knew Vargas had men keeping constant watch on the roads into and out of Santa Fe.

The trio took a road that ran parallel to the river through town. Along the road and every cross street, everything was activity. The roads were crowded with wagons and pedestrians. There seemed to be a hundred stores. Every other sign offered "seegars and whiskey." Though Rab Sinclair had never learned to read or write, he recognized these words when he saw them on signs.

Boys in caps carried stacks of newspapers and sold them on the corners. Soldiers walked the boardwalks among lawyers and businessmen. Freight wagons, either bringing goods into Santa Fe or taking them out, choked many of the streets. And everywhere there seemed to be construction, either new buildings going up or old buildings coming down. St. Michael's College and the Loretto Academy, one a high school and college for boys and the other a girls' academy, meant that down by the river there were young many young people coming and going to lectures.

"Seems like the place is busier every time I come here," Rab noted.

On the north side of the river, construction continued well away from the main part of the town. Clusters of houses sat among the hills to the east. But below the river, the town came to an abrupt end beyond the place where, in the coming years, the railyard would be built. There were just a few houses out that way, and the trees lining the river quickly gave way to sandy and grassy flats stretching far off to the west and dotted with round juniper bushes. And beyond the flats, a line of mountains separated earth from sky on the distant horizon. Rab knew that over among those mountains was the Rio Grande, making its way toward Old Mexico from the high mountains of Colorado Territory. The Santa Fe River would meet the Rio Grande at the edge of the flats.

As they left the city behind, Rab watched the sandy ground for tracks. There was no road here, and if Caleb or one of the others had ridden into town for provisions and come this way, Rab felt certain he would eventually spot a hoof print. Vazquez and Evangeline knew what he was watching for, and so they kept the spare mounts and pack mules back a ways to give Rab room to find tracks.

"There it is," he said, drawing reins on the blue roan.

He sat looking at it. Just a white spark on a dirt colored rock, but for someone who knew what they were looking for, it might as well have been a sign that read "seegars and whiskey."

Rab dropped from his saddle and knelt down beside the white mark. It gave him a starting place, and he began looking around in a circle extending out from the white spark. Several feet away, he found a clear hoof print in the sand, and another. Rab whistled and the roan walked over to where he was standing. He took the reins and led the horse. Vazquez and Evangeline held their horses where they were, watching Rab pick his way along. He disappeared behind a juniper and then came out the other side.

"Moseying through here," Rab said. "It's Caleb's horse."

He'd seen the tracks all over the ranch and

recognized them with ease. He recognized the length of the steps and could see when the horse was at a trot or when it was going at an easy walk. The tracks here suggested an uneasy walk.

"Reluctant," Rab said, more to himself than the others.

"What's that?" Evangeline called to him.

"I would call it a 'reluctant' gait," Rab said. "Horse and rider who made these tracks were in no hurry. These are the tracks he made coming into the town. I don't see any that show him going back to the camp, but they won't be far from here."

"No question about it?" Evangeline asked. "Definitely Caleb?"

Rab nodded, studying the tracks at his feet.

"Definitely Caleb's horse. No question. I assume he's riding his own horse."

Rab continued to walk, pulling Cromwell behind him. Vazquez and Evangeline followed at a slow distance. The tracks led south of the river now, almost due south. Rab had expected to follow the tracks along the river, thinking it most likely they would have camped there. The Santa Fe seldom ran with a decent flow nor any depth, but there was a little water running in it now, enough to water horses, anyway. But the tracks now suggested they were camped somewhere away from the river.

"The problem with a reluctant gait is that he's meandering all the hell over the place," Rab said. The trail he'd followed so far wound around juniper bushes and now seemed to be dropping well away from a straight line toward a low hill in the distance. It was going to take some time to follow this trail to any sort of conclusion, and Rab said so.

"Still early in the day," Vazquez said. "We've got nothing but time."

Rab nodded.

"If they decided to drop south to Albuquerque, they might well extend their jump on us to three days before we figure that out," Rab said.

"Do you have a suggestion of something better to do than just following these tracks?" Vazquez asked.

Rab pointed west, back toward the river.

"Three or four miles that way, right on the riverbank, there's a trading post," Rab said. "It's run by some Indians from the pueblo on the other side of the Rio Grande. Why don't you ride up to the trading post and see if anyone there has seen Matty Rio and his outfit. After you've learned what you can learn there, ride south and I expect you'll run right into us. This trail ambles all the hell over the place, but it's running generally southwest."

Vazquez nodded.

"I'll catch up in an hour or so. Four miles?"

"About that," Rab said.

***

When Caleb returned with the supplies, Matty Rio was eager to gather new information.

Chavez and Eduardo went to work cooking up the beans and bacon, but Matty led Caleb away from the camp. He was nervous in a way that Caleb had never seen him before.

"It's gotten bad with Wool," Matty Rio said. "His dander's up something awful. You saw the way he shot Joe."

"I saw it," Caleb said, looking darkly back toward the camp. Chavez and Eduardo were busy getting the fire started back up, but Bud Woolery was skulking around with his shoulders pushed forward and his head drooping so that his chin touched his chest.

The outfit was somehow transformed into something it had not been before, and the transformation disturbed Caleb.

Matty Rio's easy confidence was replaced by apparent desperation.

Wool, always wound too tight, seemed like a spring ready to burst.

Chavez was grumpier than usual, and Eduardo took his cue from Chavez.

And, of course, the most solid man in the outfit was lying dead behind some juniper bushes.

"We'd better bury him, or move our camp," Caleb said. "He's going to start to stink soon, and that'll draw coyotes."

"Yeah," Matty Rio said. "We can pile rocks on him or something. But that ain't my worry. Wool's about to break. We need to figure something out in a hurry. This whole thing has gone sour on us, and we've got to get it back."

Caleb swallowed hard. The entire way into town and all the way back, his one thought was that he'd made a terrible mistake. He had no business here with these people. But he couldn't leave, not without Rab's horses.

And now, the leader of the outfit was standing in front of him talking about how the whole thing was out of control.

"Did you hear anything in town about the stagecoach robbery?" Matty Rio asked.

"Nope," Caleb said. "But I didn't go around asking anybody, either."

"What's out here?" Matty Rio asked. "Is there anything close to us?"

"What do you mean?" Caleb asked.

"Houses? Ranches? Maybe some cattle we can make off with and sell somewhere."

Caleb sighed heavily and tried to think.

"Yonder that way is the Rio Grande," he said. "I've been through here once before with Rab. The Rio Grande takes us straight to Albuquerque. There's a fort down that way, Fort Craig. We've taken cattle there before. I used to live down on the Rio Grande, close to there."

"I'm thinking something closer than Albuquerque," Matty said. "Something we might do quick."

Caleb shrugged his shoulders and shook his head.

"There ain't no houses out this way, not until you get right up to the town," Caleb said. "On the other side of the Rio Grande is an old Indian pueblo."

"They might buy some stolen cattle from us," Matty Rio said hopefully.

Caleb shook his head.

"I don't think they would, not any local cattle, anyway. But there's no cattle out this way, anyhow. The only thing out this way, them Indians across the Rio Grande, they've got a little trading post between here and

Santa Fe, up on the Santa Fe River. Rab and I went there once."

"A trading post?" Matty said, his interest piqued.

"Just a little one," Caleb said.

"Why did you ride all the way into town if there's a trading post so close to us?" Matty asked.

The truth was, Caleb went past the trading post because he was in no hurry to get back to camp. He went into Santa Fe so that he would be away from Matty Rio and Wool and the other two as long as possible.

"I didn't want anyone there to recognize me and realize we were camped out this way," Caleb said. It was a lie, but it was a good lie.

"Well that's smart thinking. What's around this trading post?" Matty asked.

"Nothing, really," Caleb said. "That's the reason I remember it. We were driving cattle to Fort Craig and we came through south of here. But Rab wanted to ride up to the trading post to buy some blankets. It struck me as odd at the time, because it just sits out there in the middle of nowhere. There's not even a real road going through there. But if you go north of the Santa Fe River, there's a forest and some deep canyons up along there, and trappers sometimes go up that way. That's who uses the trading post, mostly."

Matty Rio nodded.

"How many people are there, do you reckon?"

"Now wait a minute," Caleb said. "Matty, you ain't thinking of trying to rob that trading post?"

Matty Rio sighed and nodded his head back toward Wool.

"We've got to do something," he said. "He's gotten dangerous."

Matty remembered a traveler up near Trinidad. Caleb didn't know anything about it, but Matty Rio realized that the signs had been there as long as he'd known Wool.

"Not that he wasn't always a little dangerous," Matty added.

A silence fell between the two of them for a time. Matty Rio glanced back at the skulking Bud Woolery. Chavez and Eduardo still didn't have a pot on the fire. Eduardo was bent over close to the wood, blowing on it to try to get the flames to jump up. Matty wondered if maybe some grub wouldn't improve Wool's mood.

"Ain't you got that fire going yet?" Matty asked.

"Soon," Chavez said.

They were all hungry and touchy, and Matty said so to Caleb.

"What we need is a good plan to put a little money in our pockets. So tell me now, how many people do you reckon are up around that trading post?"

Caleb rolled a rock under the toe of his boot, looking at the ground.

"It's been some time since I was there," he said. "I remember they had a couple of little adobe huts outside the trading post. It seems to me that there was one family, a man and a woman. They had a couple of sons, and maybe a daughter or two."

"So you're talking five or six?" Matty said.

"That seems right," Caleb said.

"And nobody else is around there? I mean, they don't have a whole village around the trading post, because I've seen that before. One trading post with a whole village of tipis around it."

"No," Caleb said. "The pueblo is across the Rio Grande."

"And they're friendly Injuns?" Matty Rio said.

"Friendly enough," Caleb said.

"Whereabouts is this trading post?"

"Ten or twelve miles northeast of here," Caleb said. "If you go straight north, you'll come to the Santa Fe River, and then it's maybe a mile or two to the east."

Matty nodded.

"Nothing to stop us from riding in there and taking whatever we want?"

"The Indians might try to stop you," Caleb said.

Matty Rio shrugged.

"Five or six of them against the five of us, I favor those odds."

Caleb shook his head.

"I ain't going to be a part of it," he said.

Matty Rio's head snapped up quickly and he stared Caleb right in the eye.

"You're going to have to figure out what you're a part of," Matty hissed, keeping his voice low so the others wouldn't hear. "You say you're a part of our outfit, but you skipped on the stagecoach, and now you want to skip on this. Either you're with us or you're not, Caleb Morgan. You need to make up your mind. You can't always hold the horses."

Matty studied the look on Caleb's face. Maybe some fear. Maybe some anger. Definitely regret.

"Of course, somebody has to stay at camp with the horses," Matty Rio said. "So I reckon that'll be you again. But at some point, you've got to do your part for this outfit, or you'll be out of this outfit."

Caleb nodded.

After supper, with nothing else to do, Caleb bedded down for the night. He was exhausted. He'd had two sleepless nights, and he knew that if he started thinking too much about that trading post and the Indians who ran it, he'd have another sleepless night.

Lying in his bedroll, Caleb kept wondering if there might be some way he could get all of Rab Sinclair's horses out of there before this went any farther. He was frightened of what morning would bring if the rising sun found him and those horses still at the camp and still with Matty Rio's outfit.

- 15 -

Matty Rio, Chavez, and Bud Woolery stood beside their horses on a little rise about half a mile below the trading post. Their horses were tied behind big juniper bushes, and the men knew that among the shrubs they would not stand out on the horizon for anyone to see.

They'd been there for three quarters of an hour, just watching. In that time, no one had come or gone from the trading post at all. They'd seen no riders out on the horizon. The only evidence of life they'd seen was a man who walked from one of the huts behind the trading post up to the wooden porch where he promptly sat down in a chair and did not stir again.

"You think he's the only one there?" Chavez asked.

"Appears to be," Matty Rio said. "I don't even think there's anyone else inside it."

"Could be others in the huts," Wool said.

"Maybe, but it's late in the day to still be inside," Matty Rio said.

They stood and watched a little while longer, Matty was keen on keeping an eye on the horizon in all directions. What he didn't want was someone coming up on them while they were in the process of holding up the trading post.

"They cook meals there," Chavez said. "Look at all the tables off to the side. If they've got cooks, there's more than one person there."

"Maybe some women," Wool said. "No offense, but I could use a change in company. You boys ain't much to look at."

Chavez chuckled, but Matty Rio's stomach turned. He liked the idea of being in charge of a tough outfit, but Wool was rougher than what he wanted around.

"We'll leave any women alone," Matty said. "And no killing. You don't know who might be out on these flats. Maybe we can't see 'em, but maybe they ain't so far away that they don't hear a gunshot. Last thing we need is a posse from Santa Fe after us."

"We wouldn't be in this fix if that strongbox you promised us was on the stagecoach," Wool said. "Don't forget that."

After another quarter of an hour, there was still no more sign of life at the trading post other than what they'd already seen, and so the three men fetched their horses and started walking them down off the rise and in among the juniper, leading them toward the trading post.

"Wool, you and Chavez work your way around to the back and check those huts. If you find anyone back there, you bring them around to the front," Matty said. "I'm going to walk right in the front door like I'm there to buy something, and check it out to see who else might be inside. When you come in, that's when we'll hold the place up. We're just looking for cash money or gold or silver. We're not taking anything else."

"A bottle or two of whiskey," Wool said.

"A bottle or two, but no more than that. And no killing folks," Matty Rio stressed. "Unless one of 'em goes for a gun or a knife, don't you kill nobody."

Matty would have liked to have Eduardo with them. He felt like four could make a bigger impression than three on anyone inside the trading post, but he had a bad feeling about Caleb Morgan. Matty was worried that Caleb was disenchanted with his life as an outlaw, and he was afraid that the boy might decide to take what there was of Rab Sinclair's horses and go back to Las Vegas. So he left Eduardo back at the camp with Caleb and the spare mounts, and he brought fat Chavez who probably wouldn't be useful in any event, and Wool who was like as not going to create the event.

Wool and Chavez broke off away from Matty, making their way among the juniper to swing around to the back of the trading post, and doing their best not to be seen. Matty Rio held his horse in place for a bit to give them time. He quickly lost sight of them. The juniper bushes were as big as a horse and grew so thick through here that it was just narrow, sandy trails between them.

From where he was, Matty couldn't even see the trading post.

After several minutes, he cinched the girth and stepped into a stirrup. As he swung himself into the saddle, he was just high enough to make out the big timbers jutting out from the roof of the adobe building.

The horse was slow to respond, and Matty had to nearly drag its head to his knee with the reins to get the thing moving. He clucked his tongue and gave the horse leg to get it moving.

And then he broke free of the juniper, walking the horse into the cleared yard of trading post.

The Indian on the porch sitting in a rocker looked up from under the wide brim of his black hat. His face was scarred with deep wrinkles that looked like canyons.

"Howdy there, Cochise," Matty Rio said, using the name of a Chiricahua leader who just a couple of years prior had signed a peace treaty in Arizona Territory and recently died on a reservation. Matty Rio didn't know anything about Cochise, other than that he'd heard the man had died on a reservation.

The old Indian on the rocker wondered if the rider intended to insult, but he chose to ignore it anyway.

"I'm looking for supplies," Matty called to the man.

The Indian nodded toward the door.

"We have supplies inside."

Matty rode his horse up to an old hitching post, evidence of its years of service showing in the large bite marks and nibbled-away bits all across the top of the post. He slid down out of the saddle and walked right into the store.

Plenty of windows lined the back and front of the store, and there was light enough for Matty Rio to see all the goods.

Flour and sugar in sacks, feed for horses, canned fruits and beans, salted meats, blankets, boxes of cartridges, traps and knives made by the tribe living across the Rio Grande. Almost anything a man could want – not just to survive, but to live in a kind of rough luxury.

Through one of the back windows, Matty Rio saw Wool dragging a woman from a hut, and his gut twisted into knots. He turned quickly, grabbing at one of the Colts tucked in the sash around his waist, but the old Indian had not yet followed him into the store.

Matty looked again through the window.

The woman was fighting, but Wool had a fistful of black hair in his grip. She was not screaming, but she was making noise, struggling against Wool, and Matty could just hear her inside. As Matty Rio watched, Wool gave the woman a hard punch to the face. She didn't fall limp, exactly, but she surrendered much of the fight.

Chavez came out of the other hut, his stolen Winchester in his hand.

Matty hurried to the door of the trading post. The old Indian was still sitting in his rocker.

"Say, Cochise, you've got just about everything a man could want in here, ain't you. I seen all these tables out in the yard. You serve meals here?"

The Indian looked up at him.

"No meals. No more. Used to serve meals, but no more."

Matty frowned at him.

146

"Well, come in here and let me get my provisions together," Matty said.

Any moment, Chavez and Wool would be leading that Indian woman around the side of the trading post, and Matty wanted the old man inside with him when that happened.

The old man stood up. He looked thin and frail, and he did not walk with ease.

"Been here a long time, old timer?" Matty Rio asked.

"It is my son's trading post," the old man said. "He is away to market."

They were through the door now, and Matty grabbed a couple of cans of beans and a leather satchel. He got a bottle of whiskey and set it on the counter with the beans and satchel.

That's when Wool came through the door with his Remington six-shooter in one hand and a thick clump of the woman's hair in his other.

The old man looked up in surprise, but if he had anything to say it was drowned out by the blast from the Remington. The shot caught the old man in the gut, and he stumbled forward before falling to the ground.

"Aieeee!" the woman shouted, and she turned on Wool, throwing punches toward his face.

Wool laughed at her and held her out by the hair, then he swung the Remington hard and smashed her in the head, cutting a gash above her ear.

"What the hell are you doing?" Matty Rio demanded. "I said no shooting."

Wool scoffed and shook his head. The woman was down on her knees now, trying to give the old man some comfort as he struggled to breathe. Wool still had her hair in his grip.

Matty figured the woman must be his granddaughter. She was probably somewhere in her mid-twenties. She was leaking blood from the cut above her ear, and her eye was swollen and red. Matty Rio guessed correctly that Wool had already given her a punch when he found her inside the hut.

"We're not taking the woman," Matty said.

Wool glared at him.

"Find the cash box," he said. His voice was like ice. "Get whatever supplies you want to take from the store. I'm taking the woman."

Matty left the argument and went in search of the cash box. It took some time. He found it hidden in a dresser drawer in a room off to the side of the building.

For his part, Chavez followed his heart. He found a leather bag and he filled it with food – jerky and cans of beans.

The old man was still alive, but he was struggling on the ground. Wool released the woman's hair and found a lariat he intended to use to tie the girl up, but as soon as Wool walked away, leaving her on the ground beside the old man, the woman got up and ran through the door.

Wool snatched the lariat and then took off running after the girl. Matty Rio was in the other room still searching for the cash box, and he wasn't aware that the girl was trying to get away until he heard Wool fire a shot outside the trading post. Thinking a posse had come up on them, Matty drew his gun and darted out into the main room, but that's when he saw the girl trying to get away and Wool giving chase.

She was wearing soft-soled moccasins and the gash Wool had given her left the woman's head spinning, and she did not run fast nor straight. As Matty watched, Wool easily caught up to her, and he gave her leg a kick as she was running, tripping her so that she went headlong into the sand. Then he fell on her, tying her with the rope.

"He's going to have his way with her," Chavez said. "He said outside that we could all get a chance at her when he's done, and then he'll kill her."

Matty Rio's stomach turned.

As he went back to search for the cash box, he grappled with trying to find where he had gone wrong with all of this. His planning had seemed so precise. He thought the others all viewed him as a leader. If there was going to be a challenge of his leadership from within the group, he was certain it would have come from Union Joe and not Bud Woolery.

But then there'd been no strongbox on the stagecoach.

And then Wool went to killing all those people.

The murders seemed to give Wool a new confidence, and that confidence seemed to make him feel that he was now in charge.

Chavez and Eduardo both seemed indifferent to Wool's atrocities. But they were also indifferent to Matty's leadership.

The outfit he'd put together was falling apart on him. If the cash box had any money in it, maybe he could get control over his gang again.

When he found it in the dresser drawer, there was a lock on the box. Rather than try to find the key, Matty found a hammer and busted the lock with a couple of swings. Inside, he found just over seventeen dollars in gold, silver, and cash. It was less money than they'd gotten from the passengers of the stagecoach.

- 16 -

Vazquez found the old man in the trading post, shot in the gut and still dying.

The deputy sheriff from San Miguel County got the old man some water and folded a blanket to put under his head. The old Indian trader was delirious and dying, but Vazquez was able to piece together what had happened. Sometime the day before, three men came in to hold up the store and shot him. The old Indian said he'd been on the floor all through the night. The old man kept saying they shot his granddaughter in the yard, but Vazquez hadn't seen a body.

While he was there, trying to get information from the Indian, the old man passed on.

It was a grim thing.

Vazquez had seen plenty of men killed. Life was sometimes harsh on the frontier, and as built-up and cosmopolitan as Santa Fe tried to make itself, they were all still living very much on the frontier.

But thinking about an old man dying on the floor of the trading post, too weak to move or do anything, and being there for a full day, dying alone – Vazquez shook his head and stood up. It was too awful to contemplate.

He took a heavy breath and decided to leave the body where it was.

The yard of the trading post was no place to try to find tracks that told any kind of a story. Though the place obviously wasn't doing much business if the old man had been on the floor overnight and Vazquez was the first person to discover the body, there were still too many tracks in the yard to find anything useful.

But Vazquez didn't see a body, either out front or out back. He checked the huts behind the store and saw nothing in there that suggest there was a granddaughter who was shot.

In the end, the deputy sheriff climbed back on his horse and rode straight south, hoping to cross paths with Rab Sinclair sooner rather than later.

***

"They've got someone on foot," Rab said. "And there are only three of them here."

It was pure chance that Rab and Evangeline stumbled upon the fresh tracks from the day before. They'd been following the tracks that Caleb had left when he'd come to town for provisions when they struck on the trail of three riders and one person on foot.

"A woman, or a child," Rab said. "Small feet, anyway. Wearing moccasins."

Rab was off his horse again. Evangeline was sitting in her saddle, the reins in one hand and the lead for the spare horses and pack mule in the other. She watched as Rab examined the tracks, following along on foot trying to read the signs.

"Whoever they have on foot here, this person is struggling. Exhausted or hurt. The tracks don't follow a straight line, it's like the person is weaving as they walk. And right here, the way the ground is disturbed, I would reckon whoever it was fell over. I can't be sure, but this looks to me to be where an elbow hit the ground."

"And you're certain these are tracks from our horses?" Evangeline asked.

"No doubt. These are our horses."

"My Lord," Evangeline said in exasperation. "What has Caleb gotten into?"

Down in the flats the temperature was noticeably warmer than it had been up in the hills. The sun seemed to bake everything, including Rab Sinclair and Evangeline.

"A heap of trouble," Rab said. "A stagecoach robbery, five murders, and now it looks like a kidnapping. That doesn't include stealing our horses."

"Maybe we should go home," Evangeline said.

Rab looked up sharply, frowning at her.

"What are you saying?"

She bit her lip and frowned back.

"Rabbie, this is Caleb we're chasing. And I know he's mixed up in something awful here, but maybe we shouldn't be the ones to catch him. You and I both know what's going to happen when we catch up to these people."

Rab fished inside his pocket for his pipe and his packet of tobacco. He filled the pipe and lit it, drawing on it and letting the smoke curl up under the brim of his hat. He did not immediately respond to Evangeline, instead thinking about what she said.

"Be a damn dirty trick to leave Vazquez out here on his own after we've come this far," Rab said.

Evangeline nodded.

"Can he track them on his own?"

Rab shrugged.

"So long as they're out here and the only ones leaving tracks, Vazquez could follow them."

"But he'd have to go back to Santa Fe to round up a posse?" Evangeline said.

"I'd encourage him to do that, yes."

She nodded.

"Maybe we should do that," she said. "Maybe we should go home and let Vazquez gather a new posse. Maybe we're not the right ones to chase down Caleb."

Rab took another draw on his pipe and nodded his head, not in agreement so much as in understanding.

"You knew where this was going," he said. "You

knew how this would end. I told you before we started out."

Evangeline smiled and nodded, a sad kind of smile and a nod of acceptance.

"I know," she said. "And I know we can't leave Vazquez. I guess maybe I thought if we came along – if I came along – there might be some chance to avoid the outcome. But there's not, is there?"

Rab shook his head.

"We can't be responsible for what a grown man chooses to do, even someone we call a friend. We can only be responsible for the choices we make. These boys – these men – they're doing bad things, Evangeline. And they've got to be stopped. Caleb being with them doesn't change that. The fact that they're doing these things with my horses and my guns, it puts the burden of stopping them on me. As for Caleb's part in this, I don't like it anymore than you do. But I warned him what would come of choosing these men as his friends. He didn't come into this without knowing where it would go."

"There's only three tracks," Evangeline said. "Maybe Caleb's not involved in all of it."

Rab nodded.

"He's involved in enough of it."

Cromwell, the blue roan, was in the line of spare mounts Evangeline had, and Rab noticed the horse raise its head and turn his ears, alert to something new.

"Vazquez will be here in a moment," Rab said. "If you need to go back to Santa Fe, that decision needs to be made now. I'll take you back. But then I'm coming back here and going on with Vazquez."

Evangeline shook her head.

"I knew what I was getting into," she said. "I knew where this would lead. I said I was in it with you, and I'm in it with you."

Cromwell snorted, and Rab craned his neck to see around a distant juniper, and Vazquez rode into sight. He raised up a hand and Rab returned the wave. As he rode up even with Evangeline, Vazquez reined in.

"Damned bad business at the trading post," he said.

"Tell me about it," Rab said.

"When I got there, I found an old Indian, I reckon he's the one running the trading post. Shot in the belly and dying on the floor. Said he'd been there overnight. Said they shot his granddaughter, too, but I didn't see any sign of her."

Rab drew on his pipe as he listened. It did not take much imagination to make Vazquez's information match up with the tracks he and Evangeline had been following.

"Whether or not there's a granddaughter shot somewhere, I can't say," Vazquez continued, "but I'd bet, Rab, that it's the men we're tracking who shot that old man at the trading post."

"I'm sure it is," Rab said. "A mile or so back, we picked up a new trail. Three of my horses, and it looks to me like they've got someone walking with them. Probably a woman. She's got small feet. Could be a child, but an older child. She might be shot, From the tracks, it looks to me like she's struggling, anyway."

Vazquez swallowed hard.

"We can't be far from where they camped," he said.

"If they're still there," Rab said. "These tracks are a

day old."

Vazquez nodded agreement.

"The old man said he was shot yesterday. Said he was on the floor of the trading post overnight."

"It's awful," Evangeline said, shaking her head sadly.

Vazquez clenched his jaw. It didn't do for a deputy sheriff to show any emotion, but seeing that old man die the way he did had turned Vazquez's stomach. He was as angry as he could ever remember being.

"We've got to find them and stop them," he said.

Rab nodded. He raised up one foot and knocked the smoldering tobacco out of his pipe on the heel of his boot, then he stepped on the tobacco and crushed out the fire.

"I've seen what I need to see from these tracks," Rab said. "With what you say, it seems pretty obvious three of this gang have gone to the trading post, killed the old man, and they've kidnapped his granddaughter. I can follow them from horseback and we can move along a little faster now."

Rab stepped into the saddle on his spare mount and gave the horse a little leg to get it moving.

The tracks were easy enough to follow. There was no deviation to them, nor any effort made to disguise them. Matty Rio and his gang weren't even good outlaws. They might as well have planted signs in the ground directing a posse to follow them.

- 17 -

Twice in the night Wool took the Indian woman into the brush and had his way with her. She squealed and struggled. Wool slapped her around and cussed her.

Caleb and Matty Rio both sat stoned face and pale through the ordeal. Neither of them had counted on a thing like this, and it sickened both of them.

Chavez, with his belly full, moved his bedroll away from the rest of the camp and slept. Eduardo was also sickened by the way Wool abused the woman, and he sat up and kept a sorrowful vigil with Caleb and Matty Rio.

The second time it happened, Caleb wondered out loud if they should do something to stop it.

"What are you going to do?" Matty Rio asked, his voice dropped to a hush. "You going to go back there and shoot Wool? Even doing what he's doing, he'd beat you to the trigger pull."

Caleb curled his lip in disgust. All the toughness had leaked out of Matty Rio. All the swagger that initially attracted Caleb. The man was no leader of this outfit. He was just a fraud.

The take from the stagecoach and the take from the trading post wasn't even going to buy all of them passage on a stagecoach from Albuquerque to Tucson, much less California. And what had started as a simple stagecoach robbery had now turned into something so terrible that Caleb couldn't even put a name to it for the shame that it brought him. Murders. Kidnapping. Rape. And Caleb was as deep in it as any of the rest of them, even though he'd had no part in the more vile acts.

"We're all going to hang," Caleb said.

Matty Rio's anger and frustration exploded, and in a flash his hand shot out and struck Caleb in the side of the face.

"You just shut your mouth," Matty Rio said. "Not another damn word from you. I'm sick of your belly-aching."

Caleb tossed another couple of sticks on the smoldering fire, and then he curled up under his blanket.

The days on the flats were getting hot, but the nights were still very cool. This night, especially, felt bitterly cold.

He did not sleep.

The sobbing from the woman kept him awake. When he was finished with her, Wool bound her wrists and ankles and slept beside her so that if she moved or tried to get away, he would know.

But even if the woman was not sobbing, Caleb did not think he would have slept.

His face stung where Matty Rio slapped him, but his pride stung more.

All Caleb thought about was Rab Sinclair. He couldn't imagine another man trying to strike Rab the way Matty had just hit him. Rab would have busted that man's jaw. But Rab Sinclair also would have never been in this fix. Caleb didn't understand how he'd been so foolish. Rab had even warned him against getting caught up with Matty Rio and his outfit. But Matty had made it all sound so good. No one would get hurt. They would have money to go to California. They could leave Rab's horses in a place where he could get them.

Stagecoaches were held up all the time. Most of the time no one cared. No posse formed up, the passengers went on their way, and the highwaymen who did it got away. Depending on where it happened, maybe the sheriff would send a deputy to try to find the men, or if they knew who did it, maybe some wanted circulars would go around. But murder was something else, especially murder of innocent stagecoach passengers.

"It wouldn't surprise me if they've got fifty men in a posse chasing after us," Caleb said.

Matty Rio's temper had subsided.

"We'll get out of here at first light," Matty said. "We'll get out of here and get out of the territory, and we'll get far enough that they won't be coming after us."

Rab wouldn't have been in this, and when Caleb looked back at it and thought about all that had transpired, he knew he shouldn't be in this either.

The Indian woman from the trading post sobbed quietly not twenty feet away, and the thought struck Caleb hard that Rab Sinclair also would do something to help her.

"They're going to hang us," Caleb said.

"I know it," Matty Rio said. "I know they're going to hang us."

- 18 -

Rab Sinclair caught a scent on the wind. Not a strong smell of smoke, but a ghost of a smell from a fire now burned out.

"We're close to their campsite," he said.

They'd followed the tracks for several miles and the afternoon sun was showing signs of giving up for the day. Rab's experience was that there always seemed to be a point in the sun's arc across the sky where it seemed to speed up, dropping faster to the horizon and hurrying along the last couple of hours of daylight. They'd reached that point now, and while the afternoon sun was still hot and bright in the sky, Rab knew the daylight was running out.

"How do you know we're close?" Vazquez asked.

"I can smell a campfire."

Immediately Vazquez drew his Colt six-shooter from his saddle holster, but Rab waved him off.

"I don't think they're still here," Rab said. "It's a burned-out fire."

As he said it, they followed the tracks into a small clearing, and Rab drew reins.

"This is it," he said.

He dropped down out of his own saddle and slid his Winchester rifle from its scabbard. But the evidence in front of him suggested Matty Rio and his gang were no longer here.

"They kept their horses here," Rab said. "Must have tied a hitching rope or picketed them. You can see the way the grass is all cropped. They were probably here for the better part of two days."

Vazquez and Evangeline both dismounted, also.

Walking around a juniper bush, Vazquez called to Rab.

"Here's the fire pit," he said.

Vazquez knelt down beside the dark coals and put his hand close to them.

"Cold," Vazquez said. "Maybe left out of here yesterday?"

Rab walked over beside him and kicked a few of the

coals over. He put his hand over the area he disturbed.

"There's some warmth here," Rab said. "The coals on top will always be cooler, but if you're checking for heat go a little deeper. I'd say they cooked on this fire this morning."

Vazquez pushed some of the top coals away and felt the heat below them.

"So we're getting closer?" Vazquez said.

"They let us get closer," Rab said. "They spent two nights here, I'd say. Yesterday they went back to the trading post, hoping to get what they could there. They came back and camped here again last night. And they broke camp this morning. Just knowing the types we're dealing with, I'd say they got up after the sun and were slow to break camp. We might only be a few hours behind them at this point."

Vazquez nodded.

"Ain't many early risers among outlaws," he agreed. "So do we push on with the daylight we have left?"

Rab straightened up and clucked his tongue, looking at the sun.

"We've got light yet this afternoon," he said. "A couple of hours still, anyway. We're not far from the Rio Grande, and good water and good grass for the horses would be a nice thing. We can follow their tracks and see which way they go. If it was me, I'd follow the river, so maybe that's what they've done."

Evangeline loosened the girth on her horse's saddle and then stepped around a juniper bush to where Rab and Vazquez were standing.

"I'm going to walk over here a little ways," she said

with an awkward grin, and Rab took her meaning.

"Take a pistol with you," Rab said. "Just to be safe."

Evangeline smiled and nodded, and went back to grab her six-shooter from her saddle holster.

The camp was in disarray.

Rab had seen enough cattle drive camps to know it was common for drovers and drifters alike to toss empty cans around, but he could not abide a camp full of litter. This one was as bad as any he'd ever seen. The campfire pit had several open cans. Glass from a broken whiskey bottle sat at the base of a large rock. They'd left behind a sack of flour, its contents spilled out in the sand. And one bedroll – though it was really just a blanket – was wadded up and pushed under the branches of a juniper bush.

"They ain't much for keeping a clean camp," Rab said, his nose wrinkled in disgust.

From behind the brush in the direction Evangeline had gone, the two men heard a shout of surprise.

"Rabbie!" Evangeline called. "You should come and see this."

Vazquez and Sinclair shared a concerned glance and they both rushed to where Evangeline was standing over an oblong pile of rocks.

"Look close," she said with a nod at the rocks.

Both men saw it right away. The rocks were loosely, carelessly piled. Through the gaps between the rocks they could see clearly the body beneath them.

"Is it Caleb?" Evangeline asked.

"It's the one they called Union Joe," Rab said, kicking a rock away from the cavalry boots still on the body.

Vazquez toed a couple of rocks away from the head to expose the man's face. The face was caked in blood, and a hole just above the left eyebrow showed where he'd been shot.

"The old man at the trading post didn't do this," Vazquez said.

"No," Rab agreed. He pressed the toe of his boot against the body. "Very stiff. They robbed the trading post yesterday, I reckon this body has been here at least two days."

"Disagreement in the outfit?" Vazquez asked.

"Likely so. Whoever shot him was pretty close. Look at the damage to the back of his skull. That's a shot fired not more than a few feet away."

Rab picked up a couple of large stone and tossed them onto the mound.

"You going to bury him?" Vazquez asked.

"I'll finish the job they started," Rab said.

Vazquez bent over and started picking up loose stones nearby. Most of them were no bigger than a fist, so it took them some time to get the body sufficiently covered.

When they were finished, Rab spent some time searching the area for tracks leading out of the campsite while Vazquez looked around for another body, expecting to find the Indian woman. But there was no sign of her, and in the end they decided that Matty Rio and his gang probably put her on Union Joe's horse.

With the daylight left to them, Rab followed the tracks leading out of the campsite.

The tracks cut west for some distance and dropped

down into a wide and hilly canyon. As they came up out of the canyon, the juniper gave way to sagebrush and grass and an open and desolate landscape. But all the way the Jemez Mountains grew and took shape in front of them.

Rab knew they were approaching the Rio Grande.

By the time the sun dropped behind the Jemez Mountains, Rab had already drawn up to make camp.

"Won't be a fire tonight," he said, looking across the landscape barren of any trees.

The two-man and one-woman posse chewed jerky for their supper, though the horses and mule had as much wheatgrass as they could want.

Night fell leaving them mostly in darkness, though the moon, already in the sky as night fell, was beginning to fill out and cast a silvery light across the open plain.

Vazquez let loose a big yawn, rolled over, and his breathing leveled off in a way that let Evangeline know he'd gone to sleep.

Rab wasn't far behind him. His eyes felt heavy and burned, both from tiredness and the dust that had been blowing into his eyes ever since they came out of the canyon into dry and dusty plains.

Evangeline, lying on a blanket close to Rab, pressed two fingers into his shoulder.

"You awake?" she asked, her voice a tiny whisper.

"Not trying to be," Rab said.

"I've been thinking," Evangeline said, and Rab knew he wasn't going to be asleep any time soon. He rolled over to face her, though he could only just make out her features in the silver light.

"Have you thought any more about turning back," Evangeline said, her voice still very small.

Rab was not surprised that she wanted to resume this conversation.

"I have not," Rab said.

"I didn't think so," Evangeline said. She was silent for a few moments, and then said, "They've killed people. If we catch them, they'll hang for what they've done."

"A lot of people," Rab said. "They've killed a lot of people, and justice is coming after them. Whether it's us who catch them or someone else."

Rab could almost hear her mind turning.

"Your daddy was a preacher, Rab. What did he teach you about God's mercy?"

Rab chuckled.

"I understand how you feel. How you feel about Caleb and how you feel about us riding after him. But this gang that Caleb is with, they're killers, and they'll kill again. They have to pay for what they've done."

"Rabbie, what did your daddy tell you about God's mercy?" Evangeline asked again.

"Mercy is the stock and trade of the Lord," Rab said, and he didn't say anything else about it. Evangeline knew the discussion was at an end, and if she was going to continue to ride with Rab and Vazquez, she would have to accept what they were riding to do.

***

Rab Sinclair was awake before dawn. The morning was chilly. He yearned for a cup of coffee but satisfied himself with his pipe. Drawing on the pipe, the orange fire inside the bowl glowed on his face. The moon had long since disappeared, and the light from the pipe was all there was. Evangeline's breath came soft and even in her sleep. Vazquez stirred just as Rab caught a hint of light in the eastern sky.

"Been awake long?" Vazquez asked.

"A few minutes."

"We should get moving soon," the deputy sheriff said. "This is our time to gain on them."

"We're less than ten miles from the Rio Grande," Rab said. "I was thinking it wouldn't surprise me if they've camped there. The river valley has good grass for the horses, water, and plenty of fuel for fires. It makes some sense to me that they cut west to get to the river and will follow that to Albuquerque."

Vazquez got out of his blanket and started to roll it up. The chill of the morning hit him when he was out from under the heavy wool blanket.

"I'll fetch the horses," Rab said.

It took some time in the dark to catch all the horses.

Being on the open plains, and knowing they wouldn't walk far after all the miles in the last couple of days, Rab didn't bother to picket the horses but instead let them roam.

In the dark, he whistled, and heard the blue roan snort back at him. He'd raised Cromwell since the horse was a colt. The horse had been a gift from Rab's father shortly before Preacher Sinclair died, and Rab shared with the blue roan a close bond.

The snort in reply to the whistle is how Rab managed to find the horses in the dark. They had wandered through the wheatgrass a couple hundred yards from where Rab, Vazquez, and Evangeline had slept. Rab kept his horses easy to collect. On the ranch, he pastured them in a fenced corral or down in a pasture where the mesa walls gave them small room to run. Though he preferred the blue roan over any other horse, Rab made sure that all his saddle horses were ridden regularly. It kept them easy to catch.

So now, even as the dim light of morning made its first serious forays into the darkness, Rab managed to quickly collect all of their mounts and the pack mule.

By the time the horses were rounded up, Vazquez and Evangeline had packed what little gear they had out, and it was still only a dim, blue light in the sky when they mounted and started toward the Rio Grande.

There was not light enough for Rab to see the tracks, but since they'd dropped down into the wide Rio Grande basin that cut a north-south swath through the center of the territory, they'd been on a rough trail, and Rab was fairly sure the tracks would continue along this trail to the river.

As the morning sun broke the horizon over their right shoulders, Rab was confirmed in his suspicions.

"We're on the right trail," he said. "These are their tracks in front of us."

He had enough experience in tracking that he could have followed any of the tracks successfully, but the task was made easy by Chavez and the big draft horse he was riding.

The horse had a long stride, and heavy, so that it left clear prints in the ground that were hard to confuse with other tracks. But they were on a trail now, and while a trail meant that Rab could set a quicker pace, he also had to be cautious not to get lazy and miss tracks leaving the trail.

The morning sun rose and cooked off the coolness of the night. Down in the flats, the sun seemed warmer and the days hotter, but it was that time of year when every day would get a little warmer. Back home in the mountains, the day was likely just as warm. They rode on for some time. By mid-morning, the peaks of the Jemez Mountains were clear and distinct on the horizon, and then they topped a small hill and below them the luscious green of the Santa Fe River valley was in front of them.

The river banks were lined with big cottonwoods, already showing their spring green. Bright green grass grew all through the river's flood plain, soft and lush, unlike the rough, brown wheatgrass they'd been riding through. With the gray mountains rising prominent behind green landscape, it made for a pretty vista.

"Let's make a fire and have some coffee," Rab Sinclair suggested.

They rode down off the hill in a line directly toward the cottonwoods, but Rab was careful to mark the spot on the trail so that they could find the tracks again.

Vazquez worked quickly to gather up some wood and get a fire going, and Rab and Evangeline unburdened the horses and the pack mule to give them a rest ahead of what was likely going to be a big push for the afternoon.

"That trail we've been following, it's an old Indian trail," Rab said. "It's going to lead directly to a ford. Hard to say what they're thinking, but if they intended to get across the Rio Grande, my guess would be they followed that trail to the ford and made it across there."

"What's west of here?" Vazquez asked. "Truth is, I've never been this way."

"That's the Jemez Mountains there in front of us," Rab said. "Beyond them, it's all Navajo country. Could be those boys are trying to escape into Navajo territory, but it's a dry and rough land through there. They'll kill my horses before they find a friendly place."

While they talked, Rab ground the coffee beans with a small hand-crank grinder while Vazquez got the coals of the fire hot enough. Evangeline filled the coffee pot with water, and they soon had coffee brewing. Evangeline also heated up some beans and bacon in a pan so that they had a decent breakfast.

"Where would you go from here?" Vazquez asked.

"I'd follow the river to Albuquerque," Rab said. "I doubt they have provisions to last them very long – certainly not long enough to find the other side of the Navajo territory. And even if they do get beyond it, all that's out that way that I know about is desert all the way to the San Francisco Mountains. Like I said, they'll kill my horses and walk themselves to death if they keep going west."

Vazquez nodded grimly.

"Do they know that?"

Rab shrugged.

"Who's to say what they know?"

Looking around at the green valley of the river, Rab recalled fond memories of a time he took Caleb hunting along the Rio Grande. It was much farther south of here, but the terrain was similar enough that he was reminded of that trip. His memories turned into a long silence while they ate beans and bacon and drank coffee.

"It's hard to think about Caleb being hitched up with this crew," Rab said at last.

He scraped the last bite of food from his plate onto his fork and ate it.

Quickly, they rinsed their plates in the river. Between them they drank every drop of coffee, but Evangeline filled the pot with water and poured it over the fire.

They packed their gear for the second time that morning and saddled their horses, and then they were back on the trail.

As Rab had guessed, the trail led to a ford where the Rio Grande flowed wide but not deep, and the horses managed to get across without having to swim. The mule was stubborn about the crossing, but Evangeline pulled the lead and Rab got behind the mule and gave it a whack with his lariat and the beast finally stepped off into the water and then determined it would be better to go across than to try to go back.

On the muddy west bank of the river, Rab easily picked up the tracks again, and they found not far from the river where Matty Rio and Caleb and what remained of the outfit had camped the night before. The coals of the fire were still warm enough that Rab thought he could get a fresh fire going just by putting on some kindling and blowing on the coals some.

"They ain't but five or eight miles in front of us now," Rab said. "And if they don't cut south in a hurry, they won't go much farther than that."

"Why?" Vazquez asked.

"If they keep following this trail they're on, that will put them all the way to the base of the mountains. It's rough terrain and not easy to get through. They could be all day just finding the right path to get them where they want to be."

Vazquez nodded.

"Then let's get on with it," he said.

- 19 -

The crack of the rifle echoed off the chalk-white walls of the volcanic cliffs. The initial sound was so clear and crisp that the initial echoes coming back and all around seemed to split the air just as loud as that first shot.

Rab Sinclair was first out of his saddle, but Evangeline was down right behind him.

Vazquez did not move.

"Are you shot?" Rab asked.

At the question, the deputy sheriff threw a leg over his horse's rump. His foot caught in the stirrup, though, and he stumbled onto the ground, holding onto the horse's back to keep himself upright.

Rab slid his Winchester from its scabbard and gave a slap to the blue roan so that the horse galloped away. Evangeline also drew her rifle and grabbed her six-shooter from its saddle holster. The buckskin and the other horses followed the roan, though Vazquez still leaned against his horse.

Rab pointed to a large boulder with two big juniper bushes on either side of it. It was just a half-dozen steps from where they stood and their nearest choice for cover.

"Get behind it," he said to Evangeline.

He put an arm around Vazquez and took the man's weight off the horse just as another rifle shot echoed around them. He couldn't be sure where the bullet struck, but he heard it smash into a rock nearby.

"How bad?" Rab asked, leaning backwards to support Vazquez's weight and side-stepping toward the rock where Evangeline was crouched.

"I'm okay," Vazquez said, putting his weight onto his own legs and then ducking down to the ground behind the boulder with Evangeline.

Rab got down with them just as a third shot rang out.

Once they were down, Vazquez put his back against the large boulder, and Rab quickly scanned him to find the wound. He was wearing a dark coat, and the blood did not immediately show, but then Rab saw the hole in Vazquez's coat down near his belt.

Vazquez pulled the coat open and winced in pain as he leaned over to see how bad he was hit.

"You're a damn lucky man," Rab laughed.

The bullet was buried in Vazquez's gunbelt, lodged right between the leather loops that housed two metal cartridges.

Vazquez unbuckled the belt and took it off. The bullet had punched a tiny hole through the belt, but the leather and the bullets in the belt had stopped it from going all the way through. It had struck Vazquez right on the hip bone, and though the bullet didn't even break skin, when he loosened his pants and lifted his shirt, they could already see a rock-sized welt growing.

"I ain't arguing," Vazquez said, stunned at his own good fortune. "But I'd be lying if I said I felt particularly lucky. This is damned painful."

Another shot echoed around them, and this one kicked up dust as it skidded across the boulder they were hunkered behind.

"I'd say we've caught up to them," Evangeline said.

They'd come some distance from the river, probably five miles at least, and were at the foot of a large, vertical cliff.

The chalk-white stone cliffs were dotted around the base with juniper and pinyon and the occasional tall lodgepole pine. Even up on the side of the cliffs, if a nook or cranny afforded it, a juniper clung as if in challenge to anyone who might doubt the hardiness of its species. But what made the cliffs unique were the rounded hoodoos clinging to the side like so many Comanche tipis. At the top of almost every one of the tipi-like rocks was a large boulder that seemed to be balanced on the point of the cone.

The rough, chalky cliffs were the result of significant

volcanic activity from a million years before, destroying and building up rock towers that were then weathered by rain and flood and harsh winds that carried away sediment, sculpting the enormous turrets and leaving behind deep slot canyons, waves of stone, and the rock-topped cones known as hoodoos.

This exact spot was familiar to Rab Sinclair. In his wanderings, he'd been here before. The hoodoos were unique structures, and he'd been fascinated by them. He had camped at the base and explored the slot canyons. Rab knew that there were paths through the slot canyons that would allow a man to reach the mesa tops of the chalk cliffs, though his recollection was that some of those slot canyons grew so narrow in places that a horse and rider could not squeeze through.

"Whoever is shooting at us is up top of those cliffs," Rab said. "How bad are you hurt?"

Vazquez still had his gunbelt off and his pants open. He touched the welt lightly and winced.

"Hit right on my hip bone," he said. "Maybe chipped the bone a little, maybe not. But it hurts like the devil."

"Can you walk?" Rab asked.

"Not easily, but I can do it."

When he smacked the rump of the blue roan, Cromwell trotted away but not far. He and the other horses found shade at the base of the cliff, and they were grazing on the grass and brush they found there. They appeared oblivious to the shooting, but Rab noted that in the shade the horses were protected from the shooter above. He had no angle to get a shot at them.

"You and Vazquez need to get over there by the horses," Rab said. "They've found a safe spot."

Evangeline narrowed her eyes.

"What about you?" she asked, though she knew that Rab was concocting a plan of some sort to get at the shooter. She also knew she wasn't going to like it.

"Up yonder, about a hundred yards or so, there's a slot canyon," Rab said. "I've climbed up through it before, to the top of these cliffs. I intend to go up after him."

Evangeline frowned. She did not care at all for the idea of Rab going up to the top of the cliffs alone. But they'd been together too long for her to think about arguing with him.

"You're a stubborn man, Rabbie," she said.

Rab took a long look up at the top of the cliffs above them. He saw no silhouette or shadow that might give away the location of the man shooting down upon them. He'd once owned a Hawken rifle, and though it was a single shot muzzle-loader, Rab's accuracy with that weapon would have given him confidence that he could have hit a man at the top of the cliffs. The Winchesters were accurate enough rifles, but it wasn't the same. With that old Hawken, Rab could measure out his own powder and give the lead ball just a little more force when he needed it. Firing pre-made cartridges, a man never knew quite what he had. And if he needed a little more, he wasn't going to get it.

He missed that old Hawken. But the destruction of that gun had saved his life, for it caught the bullet intended for him.

Of course, it did not matter what gun he had or did not have if he couldn't see a target to shoot at.

The tall cones of the tent-shaped rocks also meant that the shooter could be positioned on the cliffs in such a way as to be hidden behind the conical sculptures.

"I reckon I'll draw their fire," Rab said. "Watch for your moment and then get over there with the horses. Hunker down and wait for me to come back and get you."

Evangeline wrinkled her nose.

"If I don't like this plan will it do any good to argue with you?" she asked.

Rab chuckled.

"Likely not."

They'd been in some fixes before.

The West as a whole, but the territories especially, was a lawless land. A good percentage of the population existed in this place prior to the United States government. Spaniards, some whose ancestors traced their lives in this place back more than a hundred years, and Indians of various tribes who had been here for thousands of years – neither group cared overmuch for the laws of the government. And most of the whites and blacks who occupied this land came to it to escape the laws back East.

So law often came down to the gun in a man's hand.

And fixes like this weren't uncommon.

Having some experience, then, in fixes, Evangeline understood that the best way out of a fix was to move fast. A lot of arguing didn't serve that purpose. So when Rabbie Sinclair said to go there and do that, Evangeline wasn't one to argue with him. Arguing in a tight spot was the sort of behavior that might lead to everyone getting killed.

"Seems to me however many might be up there, only one is shooting at us," Rab said. "In that moment that he has to drop the lever to chamber a new round, that's the time to make a dash."

"Got it," Evangeline said.

Vazquez nodded, slinging his gunbelt over his shoulder and buckling it under the other arm. He buttoned his pants back up. Painful as it was, he adjusted his position so that he could get quickly to his feet and make a run.

Rab reached into his pocket and drew out his tobacco and pipe. He struck a match and lit the tobacco, puffing a couple of times on the pipe to get it going.

In spite of herself, Evangeline cracked a smile at him.

Rab Sinclair's easy confidence with everything he did was what attracted Evangeline to him. He did not get flustered. He seldom got angry. He just seemed to know that whatever came along he could handle.

With the pipe going, Rab held the bowl with one hand and picked up his Winchester with the other.

Then he stood up.

He took a couple of steps away from the boulder so that he was out in the open, standing on the path where they'd been with the horses when the first shot rang out.

Rab didn't stop. He kept walking. He wasn't overly quick, but he also didn't linger.

Another rifle shot snapped through the air.

Evangeline sprang from her spot behind the boulder and darted toward the base of the cliffs. Vazquez, hopping on one foot and almost dragging the injured leg, made his way.

The bullet kicked up dirt about five paces from where Rab was walking.

He'd reasoned through his action.

When they shot Vazquez, the three riders had been sitting their horses, not moving at all. Rab was taking a moment to look ahead and wondering if Matty Rio and his gang had gone to the tops of the cliffs. Rab knew they would have had to abandon the horses to do that, and so he was looking for signs that they might have turned around.

The shooter had time to take his aim and get off a shot.

But the subsequent shots had been well off target.

So Rab figured the distance and the skill of the shooter would make him safe enough to make a target of himself, so long as he didn't stand still.

He just needed to not get hit by the first shot.

So he lit his pipe and made himself a target, and that bought Evangeline and Vazquez a moment.

Now Rab made a dash to the safety of the base of the cliffs, and just in time as another rifle crack sent a bullet a damn sight closer than the previous.

Rab threw his back against the rough stone.

In safety, he took another draw on the pipe and then tapped the bowl against the stone cliff, knocking the burning tobacco to the gray dirt. He stepped on it to crush it out, and then he put his pipe back in his pocket.

"Matty Rio!" Rab shouted, his voice echoing off the opposite cliffs. "You hear me?"

He waited a moment for an answer, but none came.

"Caleb Morgan!" Rab shouted. "Tell them boys your with to throw down their guns and come down here and surrender."

Again, no answer came from the cliffs above.

Rab checked to make certain he still had a round chambered in the Winchester, and then he started toward the slot canyon that would take him to the top of the cliffs.

- 20 -

Facing east, looking out over the canyon full of hoodoos, Matty Rio could see the peaks of the mountains above Santa Fe. Beyond those mountains, farther to the east, there was Las Vegas. North of there, Trinidad in Colorado Territory.

From the cliff, it seemed such a short distance he'd come. Beyond those distant mountains, he could almost see his starting point, and that was enough to drive Matty Rio to tears. He'd had so many plans. He'd put together an outfit. They'd done all the right things. Their plan was perfect. And then, all because there was no bank money on that stagecoach, everything fell apart before they ever really got started.

Matty was sitting in the shadow of a squat juniper, his back against the rough surface of a white boulder. The bush gave him a little relief from the heat of the afternoon. The sun seemed hotter today than it had been the day before.

Bud Woolery wiped sweat off his forehead. He was prone against the ground, lying across the rock precipice of the cliffs. He rolled onto his back and pushed himself into a crouching position. His Winchester in his hand, he scurried away from the ledge before standing up straight and walking to where Matty was sitting.

"I shot one of 'em, but he ain't dead," Wool said. "Now they've gone to cover where I can't get a shot on 'em."

"Can you keep 'em pinned down?" Matty Rio asked.

"I reckon they're pinned. They ain't showin' their heads anyway. And I'll be damned if one of 'em ain't a woman."

"A woman?" Matty Rio said, wrinkling his brow into a frown of consternation. "Why in hell would they have a woman? Is it even a posse?"

"It's a posse come to get them horses back," Wool said. "Rab Sinclair is on that blue roan of his. I can recognize that horse, at least. Maybe they don't care about us and just want the horses."

"Sinclair. Is he the one you shot?" Matty Rio asked.

"Nope. Shot another one."

"How many are there?"

"Three of 'em," Wool said.

"Three?" Matty Rio asked, and he jumped up from his spot in the shade. "There can't be just three."

"That's all there is," Wool said. "Three of 'em. Sinclair. A woman. And the feller I shot."

Matty moved up to the ledge and looked over. He didn't see anything.

"Surely they didn't send a posse of just three. You killed all them folks. Half the law in the territory ought to be riding after us."

Wool shrugged.

"I watched 'em riding up. You can see for three miles or better. There ain't nobody else out there. It's just the three of them."

Matty chewed on his lip, still looking out over the ledge.

"We ought to be able to deal with three of them," he said.

Right now Matty Rio wished he had the rest of his outfit with him, but Chavez and Caleb Morgan were down below with the horses in a small box canyon.

When they first arrived at the volcanic cliffs, Bud Woolery right away saw the potential for ambush. All of them in the outfit believed they were being trailed, though they'd not yet seen any sign of pursuit. They found the path that would take them to the top of the cliffs – a path marked clearly by the wash of centuries of floods – and they started up with the horses. But the slot canyon grew narrow, too narrow for the horses to pass, and so they backed out of the canyon and found a place where Caleb could hole up with the horses. But Matty Rio was nervous about leaving Caleb alone, so he assigned Chavez and his shotgun to watch over Caleb. Wool didn't want the woman left with them. He suspected Caleb and Chavez would let her loose.

With Caleb and Chavez in a box canyon about a mile away, Matty Rio, Wool, Eduardo, and the Indian woman made their way to the tops of the cliffs. And there they waited, ready to dry gulch the posse.

Farther along the mesa top, down among the junipers that offered the only shade, Eduardo was sitting with Wool's Indian woman. They didn't bother to tie her up or gag her. The woman was cowed. Probably cowed before Wool ever dragged her out of that hut. Whatever difficult life she'd lived had prepared her well enough for the likes of Wool to come along and snatch her from a hut and use her the way he had. She gave Matty a bad kind of feeling, a sorrowful feeling. If she gave any sign of emotion, she just seemed to be grateful to have a horse to ride instead of having to walk.

Matty was angry at Wool for killing them folks at the stagecoach. And he was angry at Wool for killing that Indian at the trading post. But he was angriest at Wool for bringing this woman along. With all their other troubles, it didn't do to have a cowed Indian woman who'd accept rough use with little more than sobbing and then seem grateful to have a horse to ride.

Some folks had nothing but trouble. Trouble courted them like flies to manure even though they did nothing more than wake up in the morning. Trouble came and found them.

This Indian woman was one of those sorts.

Matty Rio guessed that probably Wool wasn't the worst trouble this woman had ever had.

Other folks courted trouble. They went out looking for it.

Wool was that sort.

And he'd brought a heap of trouble onto the rest of the outfit with his loose gun play. But three in the posse? If they had to have trouble, Matty Rio figured that was just the right amount of trouble to have.

"You're going to have to tie up that Indian woman," Matty Rio said.

"Eduardo can look after her," Wool said.

"I'm going to take Eduardo with me," Matty Rio said. "If there ain't but three of them, me and him can go back down to the base of the canyon and do for them. Or push them out where you can do for them from up here."

Wool nodded.

"Yep, that's a plan," Wool said, excited at the prospect. "You draw them out and I'll get a shot on them."

"Better tie up that woman," Matty Rio said again. "You don't want her running off while nobody's watching her."

Wool nodded and started toward Eduardo and the woman.

"You keep an eye over that ledge and make sure they don't break cover," he said.

Matty Rio returned to the precipice to keep a watch.

Even though he'd fired shots at Rab Sinclair, Wool never realized that Sinclair was making his way toward the slot canyon.

Matty Rio craned his neck to try to look past the hoodoos. He wasn't exactly sure where Sinclair, the woman, and the other man were supposed to be. But as long as they didn't appear in the canyon below him, he wasn't worried about them.

As Matty Rio stood watching over the canyon, a rifle shot from behind startled him, and Matty spun around, leveling the Winchester.

He saw Eduardo first, a look of shock on his face as he scrambled backwards. Bud Woolery stood not far from where Eduardo was moving, his Winchester held straight out in one hand. The Indian woman was sprawled on the ground.

"What in hell did you do?" Matty Rio shouted, storming away from the ledge toward where Bud Woolery was poking the woman's body with the barrel of his rifle.

"I ain't got no rope," Wool said with a grin.

Matty stopped just part of the way. He didn't want to walk closer.

"Come with me," he said to Eduardo. "Bring your rifle."

Eduardo did not answer, but he looked at the ground where the Indian woman's body was leaking blood from her head. He'd dropped his rifle when Wool, without warning, shot the woman.

Wool laughed.

"He don't want to get close to the body," Wool said.

He bent over and picked up the rifle and tossed it to Eduardo.

"Come on, now," Matty Rio said.

Wool returned to the white, rocky ledge and waited, and Matty Rio and Eduardo started down the rough trail that dropped down from the mesa top. There at the top, the trail was steep and almost all washed away. This was the path the water took when the big rains dumped on the mountains and the water rushed down off the mesa. Steep, and smooth, but with a few pinyons – the root systems all exposed where hundreds of years worth of runoff had swept away all the dirt.

As they descended, they used the exposed roots of the pinyons as handholds, skidding their feet along the smooth rock surface until they found purchase, and then stepping a little lower.

"Goin' up is almost easier than going down," Matty Rio said, wiping his shirt sleeve across his face to dry away the sweat.

"He's a bad man," Eduardo said.

Eduardo, who joined the outfit only because he was a friend to Chavez and went where Chavez went and did what Chavez did, was a man of few words. But when he spoke, he said what he knew to be true.

"Well, he's our bad man," Matty Rio said. "So I guess that says something in his favor."

Eduardo shook his head.

"He'll kill us all before this is finished," Eduardo said.

Eduardo kept his thoughts to himself, what few there were, but he was not oblivious to the things that were taking place in the outfit. While Eduardo was keeping watch on the ledge overlooking the stagecoach and Wool was down there killing folks, Chavez's pal determined that Wool was a lunatic. The man killed indiscriminately and enjoyed doing it. He knew, even on that ledge overlooking the stagecoach and the slaughter taking place down on the road, that Wool would get them all killed.

"Naw, he won't," Matty Rio said, scooting himself a little farther down. But he didn't know for sure.

***

Rab Sinclair stepped easily through the narrow canyon. In places, the rough white walls of the canyon touched both shoulders as he squeezed through. In other places, it opened wide.

The path up through the slot canyon was better marked than many roads Rab had traveled. Water from heavy rains flooded through the canyon created by volcanic gas. The path was littered with hundreds of rocks and small boulders, most worn smooth. Rab didn't know anything about volcanoes or what trauma took place in the world a million years before. But as a student of the world, he knew that whatever created these unique stone structures must have been powerful.

The canyon rolled in waves so that his visibility was limited out in front of him. But in places along the trail, very narrow, hollow spaces rose straight to the top of the mesa. And in these places, or when he was near them, Rab could hear voices above him. They echoed with a hollow, tinny sound, but he could almost make out a few words as the sound bounced along the close walls until it reached him.

So he was careful with each placement of his feet that he did not knock a stone or bang the barrel of his gun. He did not give himself away, but he also did not want those above him to figure out that he was marking their location by the echoes of their voices.

What he knew for sure was that the men above him were making their way down from the cliffs.

As he continued along the narrow part of the canyon, Rab came to a place where an enormous slab of rock had fallen over, blocking the path except for a tight squeeze against the canyon wall. A man could get through there, but he would have to squat or maybe even crawl.

Rab stopped walking and took a few steps back behind one of the waves of stone where he would be completely hidden from view of someone coming through that squeeze.

If Matty Rio wanted to come to him, Rab Sinclair was happy to wait for the meeting.

***

For some time, Rab heard no more voices echoing through the hollow tubes of stone. But after a while, he began to catch other noises. Distant and faint at first, but then growing louder. A rifle barrel banging against stone. A kicked rock. A slip of a foot.

These noises came from farther along the slot canyon.

Whoever was coming down from above was getting nearer to him now.

And then he heard them, scraping their way through the squeeze below the slab of volcanic rock. Gunmetal against rock. Brogans sliding along the sandy path.

One of the men was talking, and Rab thought he

recognized the voice as Matty Rio's.

"I'll tell you what, ducking under that rock ain't an easy way to go. I'd just as soon be riding on an open trail than have to duck under something like that."

Matty Rio gave the huge slab of rock a shove as Eduardo came out the opening.

"I reckon it's sturdy enough, but you can't help but think of it falling down while you're under there. That would smash you flat," Matty Rio said with a laugh.

Sinclair did not know who Matty Rio was talking to, but he knew that it might be Caleb Morgan. And in that moment, he wondered if he'd be able to pull the trigger on the boy. But the moment passed, and Rab drew up his Winchester rifle and then stepped out from behind the wave of volcanic rock.

"Throw down them guns," Rab Sinclair said.

Eduardo saw Rab step out from behind the rock wall. Matty Rio had his back to Rab, still facing the stone slab he'd crawled under. Matty looked back over his shoulder and did the only thing that came to mind. He dove back toward the hole, dropping his Winchester rifle, and scrambled back up the path he'd just come.

Rab might have stopped him, but Eduardo – who was facing Sinclair – had a different instinct.

Rather than flee, Eduardo thought to bring up his rifle and squeeze the trigger. But inexperienced in gun play, and panicked from his worries that they were all about to suffer the consequences of Wool's wanton murders, the actual order of Eduardo's movements was to squeeze the trigger before he brought up his rifle.

A wild shot ricocheted off the stone wall, and

bounced across the slot canyon, scarring the walls on both sides.

Rab Sinclair ducked his head instinctively, but he only hesitated for a moment.

Eduardo jumped when the shot fired, but he worked the action on the Winchester, chambering another round.

Too late, though.

Rab cleared the ten feet between him and Eduardo in a moment.

He spun his rifle in his hands as he closed the distance and smashed the buttstock into Eduardo's knee. In a fluid motion, Sinclair brought the rifle butt into Eduardo's nose, breaking it and spewing blood.

Eduardo dropped his rifles before crashing to the ground.

Maybe it was unnecessary, but Rab dropped the rifle butt into the back of Eduardo's head, smashing his face against the rock path and knocking Chavez's pal unconscious.

Sinclair dropped to his knee and fired a shot into the squeeze below the collapsed rock slab just as Matty Rio scurried out the other side.

Two Winchester rifles were on the ground beside Eduardo. Rab knew right away that both guns belonged to him. He always notched a mark in his rifle stocks because he loaned the guns out to hired hands on cattle drives, and he liked to have proof of ownership if one of them forgot the loan.

Unconcerned that Matty Rio would come back any time soon, Rab leaned his own rifle against the stone wall of the slot canyon and then lifted Eduardo by the back of his shirt, dragging him a ways back down the canyon. The man's face leaked a trail of blood, and Rab dropped him in a heap.

Rab had no rope, so he used his knife and cut a long strip from Eduardo's own shirt, and he used that to bind the man's hands behind his back. He searched Eduardo and took a knife off the man. He also removed Eduardo's brogans. The rocks and pebbles through the slot canyon would make for painful, slow-going if he woke up and managed to find his legs enough to try to make an escape.

With his hands full of rifles and shoes, Rab slowly slid his way through the squeeze under the slab of volcanic stone through which Matty Rio had slid. The squeeze was no longer than twenty yards, but it was cramped and difficult. At the opposite end of it, Rab stopped and gave a good look around.

At this end of the squeeze, the slot canyon opened up into a wider canyon. Here and there, tall lodgepole pines rose up toward the sky, juniper and pinyon clung to the little bit of soil that could be found in crevices.

With the wider canyon, there were more places where Matty Rio might be hiding – large boulders were scattered all over, ledges that would be easy enough to get to.

Sinclair repeatedly worked the lever on the two Winchesters he'd taken off Eduardo and Matty Rio, emptying the cartridges onto the ground.

He tossed Eduardo's shoes out into the open canyon, hoping that if Matty Rio was out there with his Colt Army he might take a shot and expose himself. But no shot came.

So Rab Sinclair scooted himself from the opening of

the squeeze and stood up against the white cliff wall.

Though he'd been here before, he did not clearly remember the trail leading to the top. His recollection was that it was a series of switchbacks and steep steps up from here, but he would have to find it. He inched his way into the larger canyon, and there he found a crevice in a rock where he could leave the two Yellow Boy rifles. They weren't hidden, but they might be easily overlooked.

He surveyed the cliffs above and saw no threat, so Rab took his Winchester in both hands, ready to fire it fast if he had to, and started following the path created by rain runoff. It was not long before he was beginning the final ascent to the tops of the cliffs above.

Fresh slide marks in the dirt showed where Eduardo and Matty Rio had come through here already. There were footprints suggesting at least three different people had gone up the slope, but Rab couldn't find any sign that more than two had gone down. He assumed Matty Rio had retreated back up the path, but he wasn't certain.

- 21 -

Caleb Morgan heard the shots echoing through the canyons around the white cliffs of the volcanic mesas.

The echoes and the distance meant that he could discern nothing from the shots. He didn't know who was shooting or exactly where they might be.

"I don't care how tough Wool thinks he is," Caleb said to Chavez. "Rab Sinclair will kill him."

Chavez shrugged.

"Si," he said. "Probably."

There was no doubt for Caleb about where his loyalties were. He kept his feelings to himself, but ever since Wool shot Union Joe, Caleb's expectations had turned to the moment when Rab Sinclair would catch up to them. Caleb knew it would mean an end for him. There was no way he could get tied up in this and not hang for it, but Caleb was just ready for it to be over. He had stopped caring about the outcome. He knew how it would all end, and now that was all right with him.

A man tied up with an outfit like this – a man who knew better than to get involved with the likes of Matty Rio – deserved what was coming to him. Caleb understood that, and he would make no argument in favor of himself. He had no argument he could make. The last few days had become nothing more than an inner turmoil as he wracked his conscience with bitter recriminations.

And so now he just wished for Rab Sinclair to catch him. Him and Matty Rio and Wool and Chavez and Eduardo. And when they were caught, he hoped Rab would keep Evangeline from coming to the hanging.

"We should go," Chavez said.

"What do you mean we should go?" Caleb asked.

"To the border," Chavez said. "Take these horses. We can sell them when we get across the border into Old Mexico."

Caleb glanced at him with some surprise. Matty Rio had been pretty explicit in his instructions to Chavez.

"Watch him and don't let him skedaddle on us," Matty had warned Chavez, speaking right out in front of Caleb. "If he tries to go, use that scattergun to put a hole in him. When we finish ambushing the posse, I don't want to be left with no horse to ride because this boy rode off with all the horses."

Chavez had just mumbled an agreement and stared menacingly at Caleb.

But now the fat Mexican was the one suggesting they flee.

"I can't steal the horses," Caleb said.

Chavez shrugged his shoulders and tilted his head in a casual sort of way.

"Better to steal the horses than swing by the neck," he said.

"We'd never get to the border," Caleb said. "Rab would catch us."

"Maybe," the fat Mexican said. "You don't even know for sure that it is Sinclair shooting out there."

"Oh, it's Rab," Caleb said. "There ain't no doubt about that."

"Even if it is, he has his hands full right now. All we have to do is follow the Rio Grande to the border."

In that moment, Caleb felt a small flicker of hope. Maybe Chavez was right, and maybe he wouldn't have to hang after all. Even a man who is resigned to the notion that his neck is already in the noose will glom to a ray of hope, no matter how faint it might be.

Caleb grew up near the Rio Grande down by Fort Craig. He knew the terrain, and even though the river valley cut right through the desert, Caleb knew the entire way there was sufficient vegetation to support the horses, and wildlife they could hunt. A dash to the border, following the Rio Grande, was not an impossible idea. They would have to avoid the towns – Albuquerque and Mesilla, especially – where the law might be looking for them.

But the moment passed.

"No," Caleb said. "We should wait here. Rab will finish with Matty Rio and Wool, and he'll come for us next. Even if we made it to the border, that wouldn't be enough to stop him. We'll wait."

Chavez bit a piece of chapped skin from his lip and then spit it at the ground.

"I cannot run these horses to the border without your help," he said. "And I'll need them in Mexico if I'm to make a start there. Run your line on the horses. We go now."

Caleb frowned at Chavez.

"Didn't you hear me?" he asked. "I'm staying."

Chavez shook his head and nodded to his crossed arms where he held the shotgun.

"Do what I tell you to do," he said.

Caleb was unarmed. His rifle was in a scabbard on his horse and he wasn't carrying a sidearm. He realized that Chavez intended to force him.

"You can't threaten me," Caleb Morgan said. "You killing me or the law hanging me don't make no difference. I'm dead either way."

Chavez spit another piece of dead skin, trying to make up his mind if Caleb was bluffing. He did not think so.

But Chavez was bluffing. He wouldn't pull the trigger on his shotgun because he knew the noise might rouse the posse. His advantage now was that the posse – whether it was Rab Sinclair or someone else – was busy with Matty Rio, Wool, and Eduardo.

"Suit yourself," Chavez said. "I'm going."

He walked to Caleb's horse and slid out the rifle from its scabbard. Then he walked to his own horse, the big draft horse, and he cinched the girth tight. He was too fat and the horse was too tall to easily step into the saddle, so he led the horse to a large boulder that he could step on and from there swing himself into the saddle.

Disarmed, Caleb had no way of stopping him, though he wasn't sure he would have tried to stop him, even if he'd had a rifle.

Chavez said he was going to Mexico, but when he left the box canyon he rode off to the northwest, following the dry wash in the canyon floor that led up into the Jemez Mountains.

Just then, a couple more shots fired in the distance – one, and then a moment or two later, another.

These shots were more muffled than the others that cracked and split the air and echoed through the acoustics of the canyons.

Caleb couldn't stand it any longer. He took a couple of lengths of rope and knotted them together with a simple square knot, and then he tied the rope about chest high across the mouth of the box canyon. It did not make for a great paddock, but it would probably suffice. The horses didn't want to go anywhere, anyhow. They'd found ample forage among the weeds and brush growing in crevices all along the box canyon, and they would satisfy themselves with the idle time.

Once his rope was strung, Caleb started making his way back to where he knew the posse had caught up to Matty Rio and the rest of the outfit. He would surrender himself to the posse and when it was all done, lead them back to Rab's horses.

***

Vazquez sat with his back to the rough, white cliff face. The rocky sand was uncomfortable to sit on, and he wasn't sure he wouldn't be better standing up and putting his weight on his left leg. But he noticed that the air seemed unusually clear. There was not even a smell of dirt in the air. The place had a freshness to it, and in the shade the white rock was cool to the touch.

"I like this place," Vazquez said.

He'd opened his pants back up to relieve the pressure on the knot on his hip bone. He shook the white sand and dust from the trail off his neckerchief and then poured some water from his canteen into it. He hated to waste the water. The Rio Grande was just a few miles east of them, but he'd knew traveling in the desert was never a guarantee, particularly as part of a posse chasing men who were desperate to get away. If those men did not follow the Rio Grande and cut west toward Arizona Territory, there could be some long, thirsty days ahead.

But the cool water from the canteen provided a moment of relief to the pain in his hip, and he was counting on Rab Sinclair to bring the chase to an end right now.

Evangeline kept an eye on the horses to prevent one from wandering out into the open.

He'd been watching Evangeline since Rab had left. She unsaddled the horses. She got Vazquez his rifle so that he'd have it at hand. She pulled some grass and used it to rub down the three horses they'd been riding. She unpacked the gear from the mule. She stayed busy with these things.

She was a curious woman to Vazquez. Outside of his own mother and some girls he knew when he was growing up, Vazquez's experience with women tended toward working girls in the upstairs rooms of some of the Las Vegas saloons. Evangeline was different from all of them he'd ever met. She was tall and lean, not at all soft like most women he knew. She was efficient in everything, like a good cowhand, and she worked hard. Her prejudices tended to run parallel to Rab's. For instance, she was quick to see to the horses. Vazquez had hired on as a drover with Rab Sinclair enough that he knew the man had an affinity for horses, and the gospel Rab Sinclair preached was to always take care of your mount because in the vast and thirsty places, a horse often was the difference between life and death.

When the first shot came, Evangeline cocked an ear. At the second shot, she turned her head and stopped what she was doing. But then she returned to it, seemingly unconcerned.

"What do you think?" Vazquez asked.

Evangeline shrugged.

"They didn't kill him with the first shot," she said. "Otherwise there wouldn't have been a second. I reckon if we hear a third then we'll know Rabbie's still not dead."

"You don't think they'll kill him?" Vazquez asked, a little surprised by her comment.

Evangeline laughed.

"Not likely," she said. "We've both seen Rabbie deal with better than Matty Rio. But I guess anyone can be lucky. I just wish he'd taken me with him. It's not good not to have someone to watch your backside."

With the two shots fired, Evangeline seemed to get more busy than before. She searched in saddle bags but came out with nothing. She went through the gear in the pack and found jerky that she gave to Vazquez even though he'd asked for none. She checked her rifle three or four times to be sure a round was chambered. She went to the horses and came back.

"Rab'll be okay," Vazquez finally said, trying to calm her.

Evangeline smiled at him and nodded her head.

"I know that," she said. "It ain't Rabbie I'm worried about."

Vazquez looked around. They were in a good spot. They couldn't be reached from overhead, and the cliff walls curved around them so that nobody would be able to easily get up on them without being seen. The spot where Vazquez sat was almost ideal as a defensive position with a few scattered boulders to provide cover, and the horses were pushed back into a place where they were well protected.

"We should be fine here," Vazquez said. "Even if we're still here come dark, I think we're in a good spot."

Evangeline continued to smile at him, and Vazquez got the feeling he was missing something.

"You ain't worried about us, either?" he said.

"No, not about us either," Evangeline said. "I'm worried about Caleb, and worried about the trouble he'll be in when this is over."

Now Vazquez understood.

For the deputy sheriff, everything was pretty black and white. It wasn't uncommon for a man to walk both sides of that line between good and bad. Vazquez had personally known men who in Colorado were lawmen, but in New Mexico Territory they rode with outlaw gangs. And they crossed back and forth between those two lives as easy as they crossed the border from one state to the next. He'd been friends with another deputy sheriff in San Miguel who two years ago had taken off his badge and then went and started rustling cattle.

Hard men who worked the law and dealt with the hard men who broke it always developed the skills that made it enticing for them to break the law, too. They might see where a poorly planned robbery could have been done better. They might know they were quicker with a gun than most lawmen. They might expect that their skill in the saddle would let them outrun a posse.

So Vazquez wasn't completely unfamiliar with situations where a man was a friend one day and wanted the next.

And a man like Vazquez just did his job. If a friend turned outlaw, Vazquez went after the outlaw because the friend was already dead.

But he could see, too, where that might be tough for a woman. Even a woman like Evangeline.

"What has Rab said to you about Caleb?" Vazquez asked.

"It's not what Rab has said. It's what I know, Vazquez. These murders at the stagecoach – Caleb and these others are going to have to hang for what they've done."

"O'Toole didn't name Caleb," Vazquez said. "And he

knew Caleb Morgan. If Caleb had been there when the stagecoach was robbed, O'Toole would have said so. The warrants I have, those don't name Caleb for the stagecoach robbery and the murders, and if Caleb wasn't involved in any of that, or the Indian killed at the trading post, then I don't see why he has to be punished for it. You understand? And it was Rabbie's horses he stole. If Rab says the word, I'll put a match to the warrant with Caleb's name."

Evangeline looked at him, considering what he said.

"Do you think Rab would say that word?" she asked.

"You know him better than I do," Vazquez said. "What do you think?"

Evangeline shook her head.

"I honestly can't say. I wish I could say he would, but I don't know that."

"Well, he won't be hanged for it anyhow," Vazquez said. "A couple of years in prison, maybe. If we get all the horses back, maybe less than that."

For the first time since they set out after Caleb and this gang he'd taken up with, Evangeline felt the lightness of hope on her heart.

- 22 -

The switchback trail created by hundreds of years of runoff cut its way along the slope above the slot canyon and then opened up to a steeper climb.

Rab surveyed what he could see above him. Mostly pinyon clinging to the side of slope before it leveled out to the mesa top. The exposed root systems of the trees would give him handholds to get up to the top. Otherwise the slope would be nearly impossible to climb. But he'd have a tough time ascending the rim and being ready for an ambush.

He stood longer than he needed to.

Rab Sinclair knew that courage comes from a place of wisdom. Men survived situations through careful planning, not arrogant recklessness. Stepping into an ambush wasn't courageous. It was foolish.

But he had little choice other than to top the rim and face whatever was waiting there for him.

Rab took a good grasp on a pinyon root and gave it a pull to be certain it would hold against his weight. He put a foot on the white rock face in front of him, and with an almighty heave he scrambled up and over the top.

He threw his weight forward and then dropped his shoulder into a roll, hugging the ground as he went over once, then twice, and losing his hat on his third roll.

The mesa top was covered in juniper bushes, the same as the ground down below, and when Rab finished rolling he found himself well hidden behind a juniper. He reached out for his hat and set it in the dirt beside him.

He'd expected a shot or two. Dry-gulching him as he came over the precipice would have been the smart play, and Rab's hope in coming over fast and rolling across the ground was that he would beat the trigger pull. But there'd been no shot.

Though the juniper served to hide him, it also prevented him from seeing anything. With a heavy breath, Rab raised himself from the ground, bringing his Yellow Boy rifle with him as he came up on one knee. The juniper still blocked his view of much of the plateau around him, but as he surveyed what he could see, Rab didn't see the expected ambush. Without getting up and exposing himself, Rab scurried around the juniper, scanning the area for any sign of Matty Rio, Caleb, or the others in their gang.

Rab soon satisfied himself that no one else was up top with him.

The tabletops of the volcanic cliffs were flat, or mostly flat, and covered in yucca plants and juniper bushes, these were a good bit more scraggly than the ones below. Up top, the juniper were subjected to often heavy winds that left them bent and broken under the constant pressure.

Sinclair took up his hat and put it back on his head and took a quick walk around. He could see for many miles from the top. To the east the tall mountains above Santa Fe – those that separated Santa Fe from Las Vegas – were just visible as a deeper shade of blue against the blue sky of the horizon. What gave them away were the still-white tops where the snow still blanketed the peaks. To the northwest, more mountains, and nearer. These were the Jemez Mountains where Rab had not spent a lot of time. But he knew there were rich grasslands nestled within the mountains, flowing creeks, big volcanic structures, forests of ponderosa pine and fir trees, and hot springs. He'd been told by others who spent time here that the mountains were rough and beautiful, but these were hunting lands occupied by the Jemez Pueblo Indians, the Navajo and even the Apache, and in spite of treaties, white men did not wisely travel through that place.

Rab quickly concluded that Matty Rio must have gone through that squeeze on the trail and then hidden himself in some crevice or behind a boulder and allowed Sinclair to pass him. He didn't worry overmuch about Vazquez and Evangeline, but he also didn't like the idea of Matty Rio being between him and them.

During his quick look around the top of the mesa to

be sure that Matty Rio and the others were not there, Rab discovered the body of the Indian woman. His instinct was to bury her in some way and do right by the body, but he was going to have to leave her for the scavenger birds and animals. There was not time to bury her.

He started to go back toward the trail that would take him back down to the slot canyon, and then he heard the tinny voices again, this time rising up through the same rock tubes he had heard them in when he was below.

It was Matty Rio and someone else talking to each other. Rab couldn't make out the words, too much echo, but there was panic in their tones. They were obviously into the slot canyon, which meant they'd gone through the squeeze, and just a moment of listening told Rab that the men were on the move and not laying in ambush.

Moving quickly, Rab hurried over to the trail and began the descent that would take him back down to the slot canyon.

He knew their horses – his own horses – were down below somewhere. The animals could not make it through the slot canyon. Even if they hurried and got to the horses immediately, Rab knew Matty Rio and the rest of his group wouldn't be more than twenty or thirty minutes ahead of him. The only question was whether or not Vazquez could continue in the pursuit.

- 23 -

Bud Woolery wasn't going to admit it to anybody, but after Matty Rio and Eduardo left him at the top of the cliffs, he started to get nervous. He didn't like being up there alone. He wasn't sure that the plan was very good, anyway.

And then Wool started thinking about how easy it would be for Matty and Eduardo to pass out of the canyon and make their way to the horses. They would never even go within sight of the posse that Wool was supposed to keep pinned down.

That's when Wool realized his friends were likely going to abandon him at the top of the cliffs, allow him to cover their departure, and they were going to ride off to California or Albuquerque or Old Mexico or some damn place, and they were going to leave Wool up there to get shot or get hanged.

And about the time that realization clicked into his mind, Wool decided to abandon his post.

He followed the trail Matty Rio and Eduardo took, not more than five minutes behind them.

As he scooted on his butt down the last a long drop before the trail started to level out, Wool heard the wild shot Eduardo fired inside the slot canyon. He stood still, his heart beating fast, and then heard the second shot – the one Rab fired into the squeeze as Matty Rio made his escape.

Startled, and realizing that it must mean the posse was in the canyon, Wool quickly looked around for a place to hide. He wasn't sure if he had ambush or cowering in mind, but hiding was his first instinct.

At the bottom of a nearby cliff, about twenty yards off the trail, the soil of hundreds of years of erosion piled twenty feet high with a slight slope before hitting the place where the slope of the white cliff jutted straight up. A boulder on the slope with a juniper bush growing beside it, seemed to offer the perfect hiding place.

Wool scrambled to it and hurried up its side. He got down behind the boulder and peeked his head up just enough that he could see the trail through the branches of the juniper.

A minute later, or maybe two minutes, Wool saw Matty Rio come into view. Matty was running, and he looked scared.

"Hey! Matty Rio!" Wool called.

Startled by the shout, Matty tripped and fell headlong onto the trail.

Wool stood up and waved his arms.

"Matty! Up here!" Wool shouted.

Matty got to his feet and saw Wool.

"What are you doing?" Matty asked.

"Get up here!" Wool shouted at him.

Seeing an opportunity for salvation, Matty Rio didn't have to be told twice. He hurried up rocky, sandy slope to where Wool was hiding.

"Where's your rifle?" Wool asked.

"Rab Sinclair was waiting for us in the slot canyon," Matty explained, working himself down into a tight spot where the boulder and cliff face met. He was breathing hard.

Wool dropped down behind the boulder and kept peeking through the branches of the juniper.

"When he comes through here, I'm going to shoot him down," Wool said, his hand on his rifle.

"Don't you do no such thing," Matty Rio hissed at him. "When he comes through, if he goes up the trail, we'll skedaddle back through that slot canyon while his back is turned. Right now we need to be thinking about getting out of here."

"Did he kill Eduardo?" Wool asked.

"I don't know," Matty Rio said. "Probably so. All I know is we crawled up under that big slab of rock, and when we came out the other side, he was there waiting on us. Last I saw Eduardo, Sinclair was beating the hell out of him."

Wool grunted.

He didn't like Matty Rio's plan of allowing Sinclair to pass. It seemed to him it was better to do for Sinclair now, especially because he was leading a three-man posse, and one of those men was a woman. He said so to Matty.

"I kill him now, and we can get away," Wool said. "A wounded man and a woman ain't going to come after us."

"Well, for one, you don't know for sure that they ain't got more posse running around here somewhere," Matty Rio said. "And for two, if you miss him or don't kill him with the first shot, then he'll have us pinned down right here until we die of thirst. I don't know about you, but I don't want to die sitting cramped behind this boulder."

Wool shook his head. He didn't like it. In his mind, if they had an opportunity to kill a member of the posse, then they should take it. But he also saw some wisdom in letting Sinclair get past them and then getting away behind him. He would be some time getting up the trail. It wasn't an easy climb. By the time he could get to the top of the mesa, they could be halfway out of the slot canyon.

And so they sat there, huddled together behind a boulder and a juniper bush, and watched as Sinclair came up the trail.

"I could hit him right now, square in the chest," Wool whispered.

"Hush up and let him go past," Matty Rio hissed back.

And then the moment was gone.

Sinclair continued up the trail, and as soon as he was out of sight around the first switchback, Matty Rio and Wool jumped up, skidded down the sandy slope, and then made a dash for the slot canyon.

They saw Eduardo's shoes and ignored them. They did not see the two Winchester rifles stuck inside the crevice.

Matty Rio urged Wool through the squeeze and gave him ample time to get out the other side before Matty even went in.

If someone was waiting on the opposite side this time, Matty wasn't going to pop out of the squeeze and expose himself. But when Wool made it out without someone jumping him, Matty figured it was safe to go through.

They rounded the first bend of the rock wall and that's when they saw Eduardo, unconscious, unshod, and bound with a strip of his own shirt.

"What do we do?" Wool asked.

"That must've been his shoes back there," Matty Rio said.

"Damn if Sinclair ain't a slick customer," Wool said, a hint of admiration in his voice. "Tie a man up and take his shoes. He's a quick thinker, ain't he?"

"Beat him unconscious, too," Matty Rio said. "Well, hell. I ain't going to tote him out of here. Let him sleep."

Wool nodded, and the two of them started back through the slot canyon.

They couldn't run through here, with the trail littered with pebbles and large stones and the slot being so narrow and crooked, but they moved as fast as they could, unaware that their voices carried up the long, narrow pipes of the slot canyon the same as the notes of a church organ.

"When we get out of the slot, you be on the watch for that woman and t'other man," Matty Rio said. "They might be waiting on us. Once we're to open ground, you run as fast as you can back to where Chavez and Caleb have the horses."

"Yep," Wool said. "Don't you worry about me. I know what to do."

***

Caleb Morgan walked slowly through open area. The juniper were so thick that the area wasn't all that open, but he didn't try to cling to the cliff faces or conceal himself in any way. He did not know exactly where the posse might be, and he did not know who all might be in the posse. But he didn't want to take a chance that the posse might mistake his intentions. So he exposed himself as best he could and kept his hands out, away from his sides. He was unarmed, but a nervous deputy might not realize that.

He came to the mouth of the canyon that led up to the top of the mesa. That's where Matty Rio, Wool, and Eduardo had gone to try to ambush the posse.

Caleb stopped here, and he stepped up onto a large boulder where he would have a better view over the tops of the juniper.

He looked all around but did not see the posse

anywhere. The rounded, white cliff faces offered dozens of little pocket canyons to hide in, and the posse might be hidden inside any of those.

He raised his head back to look at the top of the cliffs, wondering if he could catch sight of the others still up there planning an ambush.

Caleb had heard only two muffled shots, and that didn't seem likely to be the planned ambush. He assumed that Matty and the others were still up above on the cliffs. His hope was that he could find the posse and get to them before Matty Rio and the others made their way back down and went looking for the horses.

What he didn't understand was why there'd been shooting but there was still no sign of a posse. Surely not even Wool would have shot a rabbit or some other varmint with the posse in earshot.

But he didn't see anyone up on the cliffs. If they were keeping a lookout, they were doing a poor job at it.

Caleb was about to step down off the rock when a commotion at the mouth of the slot canyon caught his eye. Two men running hell for leather and breaking into the open. They were about three hundred yards away. No question that the one was Matty Rio. His black suit and spiffy clothes were easily recognizable, but Caleb had to squint to try to make out the other one. He couldn't see if it was Eduardo or Wool.

In the same instant that he recognized Wool, he also realized that Bud Woolery was raising up his rifle.

In a split second all three things happened: Caleb saw the puff of white smoke, and then at the same moment that he heard the crack of the rifle, Caleb felt the punch of the bullet take him off his feet. He crashed to the ground, and the thud from falling off the boulder and hitting the hard packed sand knocked all the breath out of him. Caleb gasped for breath, but all he heard was a sick wheezing, and no breath came. Tears began to fill his eyes and run out over the corners. On his back in the sand, looking up at the bright sun and blue sky, Caleb wondered if he was dying.

He couldn't get a breath.

- 24 -

"That was a damn sight closer to us," Vazquez said.

Evangeline frowned. She did not know the terrain here, but she couldn't understand why they would have heard shots deeper in the canyon and then heard another shot down lower, closer to them. It seemed that whoever was up on the cliff shooting down at them had somehow gotten past Rab and was now down below.

"I should go and check it out," Evangeline said.

Vazquez chuckled.

"No you shouldn't," he said. "And you know that you

shouldn't. But I reckon it's about as useful to try to stop you as it would have been to try to stop Rab from going up there in the first place."

Evangeline shrugged and raised her brows at him. She knew among their friends that she had a reputation for being just as stubborn as Rabbie Sinclair was.

"Will you be all right here by yourself?" she said.

Vazquez shrugged. He gave a glance at the horses.

"If they go to move out of here, I'll have a time trying to stop them," Vazquez said. "But I ain't worried about being in a shootout, if that's what you mean. I can hold my own."

Evangeline nodded.

"I'll be back," she said. "You just hang tight."

Vazquez didn't bother to say anything, though he thought it was a bad idea that she would go.

He watched her as she made her way out of the little pocket canyon where they were, and then he took a deep breath and sighed heavily.

His hip still hurt like the devil. But as it is with any injury that isn't too serious, it was starting to get better. Not that the pain was any less, but Vazquez's ability to suffer through the pain was improving. He planted his rifle butt into the ground and pulled himself up with his hand around the barrel. It was tough getting to his feet, and he hobbled along a little ways, coming to rest against one of the rough cliff walls.

Vazquez took a look at the horses. Obviously, the runoff collected down in this pocket canyon, for there was a little bit of grass there to keep them busy. They'd been ridden pretty hard for several days now, and he thought they probably wouldn't wander even if there was nobody to keep a watch on them. And if they did wander, they wouldn't go too far. So Vazquez left his britches unbuttoned but tied some twine to the back of his britches and wrapped it over his shoulders like a pair of suspenders. His trousers secured to save him from the potential embarrassment of losing his pants in a gunfight, the deputy sheriff hopped along beside the canyon wall in pursuit of Evangeline.

If anything bad happened to her, Vazquez wanted to make certain it happened to him, too. He didn't want to face Rab Sinclair if Evangeline was killed while he should have been with her.

***

Caleb Morgan caught his breath after a moment, but it made little difference.

He'd been shot bad, and he knew it. The bullet struck him in the chest, and knocked him to the ground. He coughed some and tried to right himself, but he couldn't seem to move his arms nor his legs. He was in some pain and the pain traveled right through him and into the earth below him so that he could not feel where his body ended and the earth began because the pain blurred those boundaries.

As his breathing returned to him, it came raspy and in gulps of air. Caleb dug his fingers into the sandy, pebbly earth, but he could not find strength enough in his arms to push himself up or even roll himself over. He tried not to think about the pain and instead tried to focus on breathing right. But he couldn't do more than just gulp at the air.

The tears in the corners of his eyes continued to pool and then run down the sides of his face. And then Caleb began to think that this might be death. The violent outcome Rab Sinclair had promised him if he rode with Matty Rio and these boys. Though he had known all this time that he was on his way to a hanging, he realized now that he was scared, and Caleb knew if he was dying in the sun under these rocky cliffs then he would die alone with no one who loved him nearby, and the tears came deeper.

He coughed and wheezed as he tried to breathe, and the sounds coming from him seemed distant and foreign.

He did not know what happened to Matty Rio and Wool, but Caleb had it in his mind that they must have gone for the horses. He was confused about why Wool shot him, but he let it pass from his mind. The why of it did not now matter.

He coughed again and tasted blood in his mouth.

He was not sure how long he was on the ground like that. Maybe not more than a minute or two. And then Evangeline found him.

She swore as she rushed to his side, falling onto her knees.

"Oh, Caleb," Evangeline said, and then she shushed him, running her warm fingers through his hair.

Caleb coughed and tried to speak.

"Don't try to talk, Caleb," Evangeline said. "Let me think of what to do."

She drew a knife from her belt and cut away Caleb's shirt. The wound was bad, but maybe not fatal. The bullet had struck him on the right side of his chest, going just under his collar bone. It had passed through him, which was also good because that meant a smaller chance of infection.

"I didn't," Caleb said, and then he struggled for a breath. "I didn't do the robbery at the stagecoach."

"Don't try to talk," Evangeline said. "I'm going to have to try to turn you to see your back."

"I rode ahead with the horses," Caleb said, and he coughed and blood leaked from his mouth. "I wasn't there."

"We know, Caleb," Evangeline said.

"Not at the trading post, either."

"We know, Caleb," Evangeline said, trying to roll his body onto his side so that she could see the exit wound.

"I didn't mean for this to happen," Caleb said.

"I know, Caleb," Evangeline said. "I know you didn't mean for this to happen. And I'm so sorry that it did."

In that moment, Evangeline saw the pained life the boy had lived. He'd lost his father to an accident and his mother to illness. The man who cared for him was killed by men who'd been looking for Rab Sinclair. None of it excused what he had done, but Evangeline's heart broke for the boy.

"It wasn't supposed to be like this," Caleb said. "We were going to California."

Evangeline pressed a bandanna against Caleb's chest, but she knew there was nothing she could do, either to stop the bleeding or to save his life. He had a sudden coughing fit, and struggled to breathe.

"They're going for the horses," Caleb said. "In a

canyon. All of Rab's horses."

"We'll get them," Evangeline said.

"I didn't kill anyone," Caleb said. "I wasn't there for any of the killings. Except when Wool shot Union Joe. I was there for that."

"It's all right, Caleb," Evangeline said.

She couldn't stop the tears that were in her eyes, but she wiped them away before they began to fall down her face.

"Tell Rab," Caleb said.

"I'll tell him what happened," Evangeline said, squeezing his hand.

"No," Caleb said, struggling between breaths – struggling with the fear.

"Tell him what?" Evangeline asked.

"Tell Rab I'm sorry."

"I'll tell him," Evangeline said.

"I ain't scared to die," Caleb said. "I know I have to hang for what I done. If I survive this gunshot, I'll take the hanging."

Fresh tears fell from Evangeline's eyes, and she did not wipe them away or try to stop them.

"You're going to be all right, Caleb," Evangeline said. "I don't know how, but we'll get you home. And you're going to be all right. Nobody's going to hang you."

Evangeline raised her face toward Heaven and shut her eyes.

"Lord, Rabbie says that mercy is stock and trade. Caleb could use some mercy."

When she opened her eyes, she saw Rab Sinclair coming down out of the slot canyon. He had someone with him. They were too far for Evangeline to make out who it was, but something about their posture suggested to her that the man with Rab was a prisoner.

She stood up and pulled her hat off her head and she waved it in the air to get Rab's attention. When he put a hand in the air to acknowledge her, she went back to Caleb.

- 25 -

Rab Sinclair stood for just a moment, looking at the boy struggling on the ground and Evangeline kneeling beside him.

"Did you have to do it?" Rab asked.

Evangeline shook her head.

"I found him like this," she said.

"I had Matty Rio and that one they call Wool, but they got around behind me and made an escape. Did you see them?"

"I did not, but they cannot be more than fifteen or twenty minutes in front of us," Evangeline said. "After they shot Caleb they must have gone in that direction."

Rab looked the way she was pointing but did not see anything. Of course, that didn't mean anything. The juniper here were so thick that they could be crouched down somewhere within a hundred yards and not be seen.

"I've got a prisoner," Rab said, tossing his head back toward Eduardo who was on the ground several yards behind, rubbing his feet. "He's shoeless and unhappy."

"What do we do?" Evangeline asked.

"I'll ride after them," Rab said. "This canyon leads straight into the Jemez Mountains. They'll either have to turn around and come back past us, or they'll have to ride up into hunting grounds used by the Navajo. If they come back past us, we've got them trapped. If they follow the canyon, either we'll get them or the Navajo will."

Evangeline dropped her eyes to Caleb.

"I mean about Caleb," she said. "What do we do about Caleb?"

Rab kneeled down beside Evangeline and moved the bandanna to see the wound.

"He can survive this, maybe," Rab said. "Be good if we could get him back to Santa Fe."

No word passed between Rab and Caleb. Rab looked at the boy's chest in the same way he would look at an injured steer or examine the leg of a lame horse. He looked around, trying to decide how best to handle this new problem. Evangeline watched him, waiting for the moment when decision crossed his face. And she smiled when she saw it.

Rab picked up Evangeline's rifle and handed it to her.

"Go and fetch my prisoner. Take him back to Vazquez and then get Cromwell saddled up for me. I want to get on after these two as fast as I can. I'll be just a short while behind you."

Evangeline took the rifle without argument. She dragged Eduardo to his feet and then walked behind him back down the canyon toward the pocket where Vazquez was waiting.

Rab moved quickly. He took the heavy Bowie knife from his belt and then walked around looking at the juniper bushes, moving branches aside and studying them. At last he found what he was looking for, and he began to chop with the knife. In a moment he had a large juniper branch that he tossed on the ground not far from Caleb. Then he went through the process again until he found a second branch, roughly the same size as the first.

"Juniper ain't sturdy enough for the job, but it's all we've got," Rab said. "The branches on the pines are all too high, and I'm in too much of a hurry to do this job right."

Rab winced as he looked at the two branches on the ground beside Caleb, and he shook his head, obviously not satisfied with what he had to work with.

"They're going to hang me, ain't they?" Caleb asked.

Rab ignored the question.

"I don't envy you the pain this is going to put you through, and if I could do it any other way, I would," Rab said.

He tilted Caleb, leaning him onto one side. Caleb bit his lip and groaned in pain.

228

Rab slid one of the branches below Caleb with the thick, freshly chopped end hanging about a foot and a half past his head.

Caleb breathed rapid, shallow breaths. He'd gone pale with the pain.

"I don't mean for it to hurt," Rab said. "But I've got to do it again."

Caleb nodded, his head spinning.

Now Rab repeated the process on the other side so that now Caleb was lying atop the two branches with the heavy, cut ends of the branches coming up past his head.

He took Caleb's belt off of him and wrapped it under the branches and around Caleb's waist and then buckled it back.

"About the worst travois I've ever seen," Rab confessed. "But it'll serve to get you back to Vazquez."

Rab stood at Caleb's head with his back to the boy, and then he kneeled down and took the two ends of the branches in his hand. He lifted them up and then started dragging Caleb back toward Vazquez.

The branches were too short, and Rab didn't have rope enough to make the travois strong. He dragged the thing back down toward the pocket canyon where Evangeline and Vazquez would be waiting with Eduardo.

Caleb breathed hard. His heels dragging in the sand, the travois barely supporting him, the pain shot through him with every step Rab took.

"They're going to hang me, ain't they?" Caleb asked again.

Rab clenched his jaw.

"I don't know, Caleb," he said. "You've got yourself in a bad mess. It's a mess I warned you against. And I reckon there's a strong chance they'll put you on trial."

Caleb winced, trying hard not to feel weak for the pain he was in.

"And then they'll hang me."

With everything said, Rab continued in silence back to Vazquez, Evangeline, and the horses.

- 26 -

Rab wasn't all surprised to see saddles on both the buckskin and the blue roan when he got back to Vazquez and Evangeline.

He set Caleb down in the shade, and the boy seemed to take some relief in finally being let down. Twice on the way Rab had to adjust the travois, and both times seemed to be more painful than the first.

Rab moved quickly. From one of the saddlebags on Cromwell, Rab found a jar of honey. He poured a healthy amount into Caleb's wounds, front and back. The fresh honey had a way of cleaning a wound, drawing out infection and sealing it from taking infection. It was an Indian remedy Rab learned as a child. It worked especially well for cuts and not quite as much on gunshot wounds, but Rab figured it was better than nothing. Then he found a clean bandanna and ripped it in half, wadding up the halves and pressing them against the entry and exit wounds. He took another bandanna, one not so clean, and ripped it into strips that he used to tie the two bandannas tight against the wounds.

Rab glanced again at the horse. The buckskin saddled along with the blue roan.

"No, ma'am," Rab said to Evangeline. "You and Vazquez take our prisoner here and Caleb back to the river and you make camp there and wait for me. I could be a couple of days, and Vazquez don't need to try to mind the prisoner by himself."

Evangeline gave him a stern look.

"Rabbie, they are killers, and there's three of them out there. I've already talked to Vazquez. He can manage to take this one and Caleb back to Santa Fe on his own," she said.

Rab gave a doubtful look at Vazquez.

"Can you ride back to Santa Fe and deal with two prisoner?" Rab asked. "Caleb will have to have a travois. That means slow going, and crossing the Rio Grande."

Vazquez shrugged.

"Caleb won't give me no trouble. And if I get worried about Eduardo, I can shoot him," Vazquez said.

Rab knew the comment was intended to scare Eduardo into further submission, though he didn't look like a man who could get much more submissive. Eduardo's feet were dirty and bruised. He sat on the ground with his hands tied behind his back. The boy's demeanor was one of surrender. He'd been beat, literally and figuratively, and his face showed it.

"What about where you were shot?" Rab asked.

Vazquez glanced at his britches, still unbuttoned and hanging loose against his waist.

"I can make it all right," he said.

Rab looked at Evangeline and started to speak, but she cut him off.

"You're not going without me," Evangeline said to Rab.

Rab started to argue. He started to point out to her that it was dangerous and they were dealing with killers. He might even have said the pursuit could prove to be long and difficult. But these were all things that Evangeline knew, and none of them would sway her when she was determined.

"All right," he said. "I ain't got time to argue with you. Mount up."

Vazquez handed Rab from his saddlebag three folded legal documents.

"Warrants for Matty Rio, Bud Woolery, and Chavez," Vazquez said. "I don't know how far you'll have to chase them, but if you run into the law or the army or an Indian agent, you should have these with you."

They rode about a mile and there they found most of their stolen horses scattered around in the canyon.

"Damn," Rab said.

In front of them was a chore that would take up the remainder of the daylight. There wasn't sufficient water nor forage enough in the canyon to keep the horses alive for any stretch of time, and Rab couldn't guess how many days or weeks it might be before he could get back to the horses.

"We can leave them to fend for themselves and likely never see them again, or we can take them back to Vazquez and add to his troubles," Rab said to Evangeline.

"Let's round them up and take them to Vazquez," she said. "He's a good hand, and it'll make it faster to get Caleb back to Santa Fe if he can put him on a horse."

"I doubt Caleb is going to sit upright for a while," Rab said. "But I'll let Vazquez worry about that."

Rab and Evangeline caught all the horses. There were seven of them altogether. In the course of doing that, they found three saddles. Two of the saddles were Rab's property, spare saddles he offered to cowhands who hired on at his ranch or came with him on drives. One of the saddles was Caleb's.

They saddled three of the horses that they found, and in the waning hours of the afternoon, they drove the horses back down to the mouth of the canyon where they found Vazquez and Eduardo.

Vazquez already had their three spare horses and the pack mule to deal with. Seven more horses wouldn't be beyond his ability. But Rab did not envy him the journey back to Santa Fe, having to tote an injured man on a travois, drive a prisoner, ten horses, and a pack mule, all while being uncomfortable in the saddle from his injury.

So rather than start immediately behind Matty Rio, Wool, and Chavez, Rab and Evangeline instead camped for the night with Vazquez and his prisoners. Rab and Evangeline took turns on watch, allowing Vazquez to sleep through the night so that he would have one decent rest before starting back for Santa Fe.

In the morning, they waited for daylight and then started back up the canyon. In the place where they found the horses, Rab searched around for just a moment, but it did not take him long to come across the tracks that told the story.

Three men with two spare horses had left the area, following the dry wash up the canyon. Nothing about the tracks told Rab that one of them had departed without the other two, though he did find it odd that three men left but only took two spare horses between them.

Rab and Evangeline rode along with the white cliffs on either side of them. Though its rise was imperceptible at first, the floor of the canyon was always climbing, even as the white cliffs continued to tower over them.

In another couple of miles, the juniper began to give way to tall fir trees and ponderosa pines and even some hardwoods, and while the dry wash remained at the center of the canyon, the trees started to build a thick canopy overhead.

Though they were always rising at the bottom of the canyon, the white cliffs were soon jutting higher into the air, and closer on each side, and the canyon – which had been as wide as half a mile – narrowed to less than a hundred yards. And soon, the bleached cliffs turned to red and brown as they climbed higher toward the top of the ancient volcano.

Other canyons, like fingers pressed into mud, ran into the canyon they followed, but all the while, the tracks followed straight through the dry wash, leading higher into the Jemez Mountains.

Rab and Evangeline did not bound forward. They kept their horses to a quick walk. Both Cromwell and the buckskin could travel like this all day long, and if the need came that they had to go to a lope the horses were fit enough to make a run.

Along the way, they found two separate campsites, both had obviously been occupied the night before. A fire had been made at the first one. The second campsite was nothing more than two empty cans of beans and some foliage cropped by a horse. No exhausted fire at all.

"It's almost like they're traveling separate," Rab noted.

Neither he nor Evangeline did much talking as they rode. There was not much to say. Both of them were lost deep in their own thoughts.

Rab's mind tended toward the task at hand. He watched for signs along the trail that might indicate a place where Matty Rio and the other stopped or broke away and started in another direction. He kept his eyes ahead, searching out points from which they might be ambushed.

But he thought of other things, too. His thoughts turned to Caleb Morgan. Rab felt a certain responsibility toward Caleb, almost like a father or an old brother. His thoughts turned dark as he considered Caleb's fate. He debated within himself whether Caleb deserved to hang with the others. And what bothered Rab Sinclair more than anything was that if he didn't know Caleb, he'd have never questioned whether or not the boy was guilty enough to hang.

Rab Sinclair wasn't the sort of man to let his

personal feelings interfere with his sense of right and wrong. A man who did that did not live long on the frontier.

Evangeline's mind took a sorrowful turn, thinking about Caleb Morgan and the tragic way his life seemed to be racing toward an end.

She knew that Rabbie would take a hard view of it. Caleb had made his choices and those choices had led to his own undoing. But Evangeline's heart was softer, and she mourned the good boy that Caleb Morgan had been. She saw an unfairness in his lot in life. Everyone made mistakes, she reasoned. Everyone made bad decisions, and most folks found an opportunity for redemption. But Caleb's opportunity seemed destined to be lost to a hangman's noose.

She believed Caleb when he said he wasn't involved in the murders at the stagecoach or the trading post. Rab seemed to believe him, too.

Vazquez even held back putting Caleb's name on a murder warrant because O'Toole did not name him.

Evangeline knew that if Rab asked, Vazquez and Sheriff Romero both would drop the warrant against Caleb. They would do that for Rab because of the things he had done for them in the past. They would do it for Rab because of the kind of man he was and the reputation he had among his friends.

But Evangeline also knew that Rab Sinclair would never ask for mercy for Caleb. It wasn't Rab's way.

"I prayed to the Lord for mercy," Evangeline said in a soft whisper to the buckskin horse. "I reckon I ain't too proud to beg to the sheriff for mercy."

They'd ridden for an hour or more without a word

passing between them, no sound beyond the horses' hooves, the chirping of birds and the occasional gust of wind high up in the tree tops. So it startled Evangeline when Rab finally spoke.

"A solitary ride can do a lot for the soul," he said.

Evangeline nodded. She was following him, so he did not see her agree.

"I reckon if I can help it, I'd rather not kill a man," Rab said.

"I know that," Evangeline said.

"But sometimes it seems that you can't help it. Your back goes against a wall, and the only way out is to take a life. Do you understand what I mean?"

"I understand," Evangeline said.

"But I've done it before when my back wasn't against the wall."

"How's that?" Evangeline asked.

Rab's mind drifted a long way back, more than a decade now.

"I hunted some men," Rab said. "And when I found them, I killed them. I did it because I was angry and wanted revenge against them. They needed to be killed. I ain't saying they didn't. But I hunted them and killed them in anger."

Evangeline nodded again, but Rab still could not see her.

"I reckon before we go back to Las Vegas, I'll probably kill one or all of these men we're riding after," Rab said. "Matty Rio and Wool. Fat Chavez."

Evangeline nodded.

"I expect you will," she said.

"The question I'm wrestling with is whether I'm killing them because I'm carrying these warrants, or in spite of these warrants."

Evangeline considered the question, but she did not have an immediate answer.

"If it bothers you, Rabbie, then maybe you shouldn't kill them. Just bring them in."

Rab grunted, but Evangeline wasn't sure if he was grunting to agree or disagree.

They rode along for several hundred yards without Rab pursuing the conversation farther.

"We'll see what happens," Rab said finally.

As they continued to climb through the canyon, the terrain got rougher. They found themselves now out of the dry wash and riding up hills and dropping into small valleys. But Evangeline realized they were on an Indian path now, and the men they were pursuing had stayed to it, too, making themselves easy to follow.

Well before dark, Rab stopped and swung himself out of the saddle.

"We'll cook supper here," he said. "Then we'll travel on a ways. Only a fool makes a fire in his camp in this country."

"Why is that?" Evangeline asked.

"A fire invites folks to investigate," he said. "The Navajo, if they're around, will smell the smoke two or three miles away. They'll come look for the source. If they don't like what they find – and they won't – they'll take our scalps and horses. If that's all they take, you can count yourself fortunate."

Evangeline also slid from her horse and loosened the girth to give the buckskin a rest.

"You mean me?"

Rab glanced up at her and gave her a smile as he picked up some dry limbs.

"I ain't saying you're the prettiest thing in these mountains, but I reckon a Navajo scout wouldn't argue with me if I did."

Evangeline wrinkled her nose and laughed, trying to work out whether or not there was a compliment hidden in there somewhere.

"Make it a small fire," she suggested.

***

After supper, Rab and Evangeline buried the fire and then continued to ride deeper into the mountains. The signs were harder to follow now, and every few hundred yards Rab would climb down from the blue roan's back and look carefully at the trail. Sometimes he would roll a broken branch between his fingers or brush aside a layer of pine straw to look more closely at the ground below.

"It'll be dark in an hour or so," Rab said one of the times when he was down from his saddle. Evangeline looked around and up at the sky, and only then did she appreciate how much dimmer the woods around them had grown.

"I hadn't even noticed," she said.

"I'd like to push on a bit farther. I can't swear to it, but I think we're gaining on them. I noticed a ways back that the tracks in the ground looked like maybe they'd stopped for a bit. And here, too, it looks like they stopped again. They had a jump on us, but I would wager we rose earlier than they did this morning and maybe traveled a bit faster along this old Indian trail."

"I can ride farther," Evangeline said.

She could tell they'd ridden higher into the mountains, if not by the terrain, then by the temperature. It was cooler here than it had been down below, and the air was sweeter among all the pine and fir trees.

Rab fished his pipe from his pocket and filled it with tobacco before climbing back into the saddle. Once he was situated, he lit the pipe and then started the blue roan moving again.

"Somewhere up ahead of us, these woods open into a great big grassland," Rab said. "I've never been there, but I've heard people talk about it. We should expect to find Navajo up that way. If these boys get to that grassland ahead of us, I expect they'll be a mite more difficult to track than they have been to now. Good chance we could lose them."

He drew on the pipe and hurried the roan up a slope. At the top of the ridge, the trail proceeded for a couple of miles before it took a turn down into a little valley. By now they were riding in the last bit of light the day had.

"It'll be dark in that canyon," Rab said. "We'll stop here for the night."

There wasn't much forage other than what the horses were willing to pick off the branches, and Rab decided to tie them both for the night to keep them from wandering too far.

He tied the ropes to the base of a big pine and then

laid his bed roll on the ground beside the pine and over the rope that held his blue roan. Cromwell would alert to any danger, but Rab was worried he might sleep right through it. He felt unusually tired.

Evangeline put her bedroll beside Rab's, and in no time they were both asleep.

Rab was accustomed to waking early, and this morning was no different. Through the canopy of the trees he could see a gray light in the night sky and knew the sun would be up in another half hour. He intended to let Evangeline sleep until there was more light – there was no sense traveling until there was light enough to see tracks – but the little commotion Rab made in digging jerky from his saddlebags was enough to wake her.

"Sorry," Rab said when Evangeline stirred awake.

Evangeline took a deep breath and stretched.

"What are you doing?" she asked.

"Just getting myself a hunk of jerky until we can eat something more," Rab said.

Evangeline sniffed the air.

"I smell smoke," she said.

Rab took a deep breath through his nose. He'd not noticed it before, but when she said something, he realized that he, too, could smell a faint scent of smoke in the air.

"Well now, that's interesting," Rab said. "There ain't but two kinds of people who would have a fire here. Navajo hunters or fools. Whichever it is, our day is about to have a start."

In the little light there was, they both checked their rifles. Rab buckled on his gunbelt, and together they walked off in search of the source of the smoke, leaving the horses tied where they were.

- 27 -

Rab Sinclair sat on a large boulder overlooking the small valley below where they had camped. Without any breeze to move it, the campfire smoke had settled in the valley, enough that he could see a small haze in the treetops that were about eye level with him where he sat on the ridge running above the valley.

A trail led down into the valley along a slight slope. That trail started back where Rab and Evangeline had camped, but rather than following the trail, they'd followed the ridge above the canyon. Rab did not want to be down in that valley until he knew who he was dealing with. Being up on the ridge gave him opportunity to scout the terrain, as well.

Down at the bottom of the valley there was a narrow little creek that made a couple of big drops. Those drops, like any waterfall, put off quite a volume of sound, probably enough noise that a man approaching would be hard to hear.

The pine and fir were thick through the whole valley and made it tough to see much, but he'd found the campsite without having to look too hard for it. About a hundred yards below where he sat, Rab could see the smoldering fire. It was darker down in the valley than it was up on the ridge. It had taken a moment, but after he located the campfire, he was able to see in the gray morning light the two men asleep by the campfire.

They'd probably fed the fire through most of the night. Probably one or the other of them had stayed awake for a while to keep a watch and used the fire as light to watch by. They weren't either of them woodsmen enough to know that the fire might keep animals away, but it would attract the most dangerous thing in these woods. If a Navajo hunting party was out this way, both those boys would be lacking a scalp now.

Four of the five unaccounted-for horses were picketed near them, and the horses were the reason why Rab had still not approached the camp. He liked the idea of taking them while they were asleep, but the horses would nicker if he came near, and that might be enough to wake one or both of them. If they woke before Rab had a chance to disarm them, it could easily turn into a mess.

Evangeline was sitting on the boulder beside Rab.

He struck a match and held it to the bowl of his pipe, puffing a couple of times to get the tobacco to light, and then drawing the smoke.

There was no easy trail down from where Rab sat. No Indian trail or deer path. But he thought if he turned himself sideways to the slope he could probably go from tree to tree along the steeper parts and make it down to the bottom of the canyon without too much noise.

The trail they had followed the previous day dropped down into the valley, and Rab figured the valley must lead up to the grassland that he knew was somewhere in front of them.

"They ain't moved since we got here. Are they still asleep?" Evangeline asked.

"Sure are," he said. "One thing I've always noted about outlaws is that they like to sleep later than folks who work for a living."

In the dim light, Rab could see what looked to him to be a whiskey bottle near the campfire. He figured it was empty, and he suspected the contents of that bottle was helping them sleep through the growing light of dawn. They'd stayed up drinking and fueling their campfire.

"So, what do we do?" Evangeline asked.

Rab chuckled.

"We?" he asked. "We ain't going to do anything. You're going to go back to where we tied the horses and wait for me. No matter what you hear, you're going to sit there and wait for me. Gunshots. Shouting. A Navajo war whoop. I don't care what you hear. You go back to where we tied the horses, and you wait for me there."

Evangeline took a deep breath and exhaled in a huff.

"I don't want you going down there by yourself," she said.

Rab nodded.

"I understand that, Evangeline," he said. "But whatever is going to happen is going to happen down there in that campsite. And I'd just as soon not have to worry about you getting caught up in the middle of it."

Evangeline smiled and cut her eyes sideways at him. There'd been a time before when he asked her to stay out of the way and she'd nearly gotten herself killed when she refused to listen to him. Today she wouldn't do that.

Rab drew on the pipe a couple of times and Evangeline watched the horses down at the campsite move on their tethers for better forage.

"Have you decided?" she asked.

"Decided what?" Rab said.

"If you kill them, are you killing them because of the warrants, or in spite of them?"

Rab shrugged.

"I've got the warrants," he said. "I reckon that makes it legal, whatever the reason."

Evangeline brushed her lips against Rab's stubbly cheek.

"I wish that whatever you do, it's not something you'll regret," she said.

Rab nodded. He lightly tapped the bowl of his pipe against the rock and the stood up, stepping on the burning remnants of the tobacco.

"Fair enough," he said. "Now go on back to the horses and wait for me."

***

Sinclair waited while Evangeline started back toward the horses. He wanted to make sure she was out of the way before he started down toward the camp. Once he was satisfied that she wouldn't be hit by any stray bullet fired toward him, he slid down from the boulder and slowly started picking his way down the long slope into the canyon.

Already the light was better now. The morning sun seemed to have picked up a head of steam and was climbing at a quicker pace, now. Soon even a couple of hungover outlaws wouldn't be able to sleep through the morning, and Rab expected Matty Rio and Wool would be awake by the time he got down to them.

Rab moved from tree to tree, the slope so steep that he had to move in this way for fear of losing his footing and falling halfway down into the valley. At each tree he stopped, leaned against it for a moment to secure his balance, and then looked down into the valley at the campsite to be sure his adversaries had not yet stirred to life. He did not use his Winchester rifle as a climbing pick, though he might have pressed the butt into the soil to give himself a bit more stability. Instead, he kept the rifle free so that if he was discovered, he could make fast use of it.

As he neared the bottom of the slope, neither Matty Rio nor Bud Woolery had moved at all. Both of them had blankets over their heads to block out the growing light.

The truth was, Rab still struggled to decide what he was going to do about the two men.

He thought of the wild mustangs back on his ranch, murdered for nothing. He thought of his friend O'Toole and the other innocent people on that stagecoach. He thought of the dead Indian woman on the top of the mesa above the white cliffs, her head shot all to hell from close range. He thought of how pale young Caleb had been, shot through among the juniper. Caleb – it enraged Rab Sinclair that these misfit outlaws had led him so far astray.

Rab's instinct was to put these two men down like he would a rabid coyote or a coiled rattler.

It would be a small thing to execute both of them. Vazquez would ask no questions. Sheriff Romero back in Las Vegas would ask no questions. No judge nor jury would care. That they were dead would suit the authorities, and everyone concerned would take Rab's word for it. If anyone asked a question, Rab could merely say that Matty Rio and Wool resisted being taken back to Las Vegas. It was true enough. They'd attempted to ambush Rab and Vazquez back at the hoodoo canyon. If he needed legal or moral grounds to kill them in their sleep, the welt on Vazquez's hip gave it to him.

But killing them where they lay, executing them with a shot to the head, Rab Sinclair found himself balking at that.

He'd done it before – killed men who needed killing. But it didn't sit well with him. It was different killing a man in self-defense, or killing a man to save another person.

One of the horses nickered at him.

Neither Rio nor Wool even stirred at the noise.

Rab walked down into the campsite, ignoring his stolen horses for the time. He moved quietly as he approached the campfire and the two sleeping men, careful where and how he stepped to avoid broken limbs or patches of brittle pine needles that might crinkle underfoot.

Their gear was spread all over creation. A pan was sitting over by the creek where they'd washed it. Their coffee pot was beside the fire. The saddles were across the campfire from where the two men were bedded down. The whiskey bottle beside the campfire still had a little liquid in it, but not much.

Between them, they had just two guns that Rab could see. A Winchester rifle, one of Rab's own guns stolen from his cabin, was laid against one of the stolen saddles. The Colt Army that Matty Rio wore in the sash around his waist was on the ground beside where one of them slept. Rab assumed it was Matty Rio sleeping beside the Colt, but he could not be sure because both men had their heads covered.

They still had a fair amount of firewood beside the campfire.

Rab picked up the coffee pot and filled it with water from the stream. He found a sack of ground-up coffee beans. He collected the sack and kneeled down beside the fire. He put some of the broken twigs down near the hot coals and then leaned over and blew on the coals until the twigs started to catch, and then Rab fed the fire with some bigger sticks to get it up a little bit.

Neither man moved under their blankets.

Rab Sinclair didn't wonder at his own actions. He knew what he was doing.

He'd come into their camp silently enough, but he knew that he risked one or both of them waking up as he moved around. He also got the fire going and made the coffee before he worried about their weapons.

Rab was giving them a chance.

It was easier to kill a man in self-defense than it was to execute a man in his sleep.

Let them hear me, Rab thought. *Let them try for their guns.*

But neither man moved.

When he had a good fire going, Rab put the coffee on to boil. He stood up and backed away from the fire.

Only then did he bother with the rifle and the Colt.

He did not know what had happened to the third man – that would be fat Chavez. But Rab wasn't worried about him, either. He seemed to have run off and abandoned the others, maybe he'd left them all the way back at the hoodoo cliffs, or maybe he'd been with them when they set up this camp and made off after the other two were drunk and asleep. Either way, Chavez seemed to have disappeared.

He leaned his own Winchester against the trunk of a tall ponderosa pine that reached high above the campsite. He knew right where it was, and every move he made after setting it down was designed to keep him in between that Winchester and the two sleeping bandits. He also slid the leather thong away from the hammer of his Colt Dragoon so that nothing would delay him if he had to draw and shoot.

Rab stood by the creek and emptied Matty Rio's Colt. That was quiet enough work. He just opened up the gate and spun the cylinder, taking out each bullet and tossing them one-by-one into the creek. But he'd have to eject the bullets from the Winchester by working the lever, and that was a nosier proposition. In the end, he decided to remove the Winchester a little ways from camp and leave it sitting by the creek. It was easier to move the

Winchester out of reach than to try to get it emptied without waking the men.

Rab found a tin cup in the camp and washed it out. Then he walked over to the fire and poured himself a cup of coffee. The water never rose to a boil, but it was warm enough now.

Then he stood over the blanket that hid the one he figured to be Matty Rio, his cup of coffee in his hand, and with the toe of his boot he flicked the blanket back off of the sleeping man's head. Matty was sleeping on his back. In the sudden light, his eyes opened. He looked dazed and surprised.

Rab pressed the toe of his boot into Matty's nose, squashing it against his face.

"Ah! Damn!" Matty Rio shouted, swiping an arm at Rab's leg.

Rab swung his leg clear and then gave Matty Rio a solid kick to the ribs.

Matty coughed and doubled up on the ground.

The commotion brought Wool out of his bedroll like a rattler. He had a long fighting knife in his hand. He'd slept with the knife under his blanket. But Wool came awake disoriented and didn't know where to swing the knife.

Before he could get it figured out, Rab threw the hot coffee in his face.

"Oh hell!" Wool shouted.

Rab reached with his empty hand and twisted Wool's wrist until the knife fell to the ground. Then he kicked it clear of the camp.

"You boys both awake now?" Rab asked.

Wool was cussing a storm and wiping at his eyes with his blanket.

"What'd you throw on me?" Wool whined.

"My coffee," Rab said. "Consider yourself fortunate. I'd intended to get it to a boil before pouring a cup."

"Well it feels like it was boiling," Wool growled.

"No it doesn't," Rab said. "That coffee was just a mite warm. Boiling would've felt worse."

Rab reached down for the coffee pot and poured himself another cup of coffee.

Then he took four or five steps backwards, only a couple of feet away from his Winchester. One hand held the coffee, the other hand rested on the grip of his Dragoon.

"You boys awake and sober enough to hear what I'm going to say to you?" Rab asked.

Neither man answered the question.

"It's important that I know you're awake enough to understand what I'm saying," Rab said. "You two are in a fix, but it could get worse if you don't pay attention. Are you listening to me?"

Matty Rio had pulled himself upright into a sitting position, but he was still rubbing his nose. Wool still had the blanket against his face. He lowered it now, displaying red skin but no serious burns.

"All right," Rab said. "I've got warrants on you both, and I'm taking you back to Las Vegas. If you try to fight or flee, it'll suit me right down to the ground to kill you both. I've spent the best part of the last two days trying to decide if I was going to kill you or take you back to your trials in Las Vegas. If you force me to kill you, that's all right, too."

Matty Rio looked around for his Colt, and Rab noticed his eyes fall on the sash. The gun had been sitting on top of it when Rab took it to the creek to unload it.

"I emptied it and left it down by the creek," Rab said. "It can stay there. I did that more for your protection than I did for my own. Now tell me, which one of you shot Caleb Morgan?"

Matty Rio looked at Wool. They'd been partners longer than anyone else had even been in the outfit with them. Bud Woolery was the first member of Matty's outfit, and they'd been together for several months. But none of that meant anything now as Matty Rio rushed to betray his friend.

"Wool shot all of 'em," Matty Rio said. "He did for all them folks at the stagecoach, and the old man at the trading post. He shot Union Joe. And the Indian woman we took from the trading post. And he's the one that shot Caleb."

"Shut up!" Wool said.

"You're a killer, huh?" Rab said.

Wool's face was red from the hot coffee. But he wore a defiant expression.

"He just named all them folks I killed," Wool said with a snarl. "I guess I am a killer."

Rab nodded. His manner was easy. He took a sip from the coffee cup in his hand. Though he stayed calm on the outside, Rab felt a visceral reaction inside. The defiant expression on Wool's face, the insolence in his tone, the complete lack of remorse over multiple murders. Rab wanted to drag the boy to the creek and hold his head under water until Wool was finished breathing. But he kept his cool.

"How many of those people you brag about killing were unarmed when you killed them?" Rab asked.

- 28 -

Rab watched them as they gathered up their gear. They did not have much other than their blankets and some cooking utensils.

Wool bunched up his blanket.

"You should roll that," Rab said to him. "We won't be a mile down the trail before it comes loose."

Wool shrugged his shoulders.

"I've gone a long ways without you telling me how to tie my gear," Wool said.

"Suit yourself," Rab said, walking over to pour what remained of the coffee onto the fire and then kicking it under dirt to make certain it was out.

Matty Rio was cowed. He hung his head and moved without thought. Rab figured both men knew the odds of escaping the hangman's noose were poor, and Matty Rio seemed to have accepted that he was heading to the gallows. But Wool adopted an insolent attitude, and Rab expected that if he was going to have to fight one of the two of them, it would likely be Bud Woolery.

"Where's the third one at?" Rab asked. "Chavez?"

"He took off," Matty Rio said. "We haven't seen him since back yonder at the cliffs where we tried –" he cut himself short.

"Where you tried to ambush me?" Rab said. "You might as well go ahead and say it. I was there. I remember what happened."

Matty Rio shrugged.

"Well, he rode this same way," Rab said. "I've seen his tracks. You boys know the Navajo use this area to hunt?"

Neither of them said anything, not feeling overly communicative.

"I reckon it won't be long before Chavez finds out that the Navajo move around this area," Rab said. "I can't see them giving him much of a warm welcome, neither."

When the gear was packed, Rab had both men saddle two of the horses. He made sure they left the girths plenty loose, thinking that if they could swing a leg into the saddle and be off and running then one or both of them might try to make a run.

He would have preferred to tie them up, bind their wrists, but he also didn't want to get that close to them without someone else there to keep a gun on them. He decided it would be better to bind their wrists when they were up the trail to Evangeline.

With the horses saddled and all the leads looped together, Rab forced Matty Rio and Wool to walk up the trail in front of him, and Rab took the horses behind him, the lead in one hand while he kept his Winchester rifle in the other hand. He did go back to the river and grab Wool's stolen rifle and Matty Rio's Colt Army, but he ejected all the rounds from Wool's rifle before they got started back up the trail.

They were several minutes on the trail, rising the whole time up out of the narrow valley, when at last Rab heard the blue roan nicker at their approach.

Evangeline was standing half-hidden behind the trunk of a tall pine, her rifle trained on the men coming up the trail. When she saw Rab walking behind them and leading the horses, she stepped out from behind the pine tree.

"I guess they didn't put up much of an argument," she said, but she was looking curiously at Wool's red face.

"Ruined my morning coffee, but no more than that."

Sinclair was meticulous in how he dealt with his two prisoners.

"I reckon it would be too much to my pleasure to shoot the two of you," Rab told them. "So you do everything I tell you to do, and you do it the first time I tell you."

He told them to hug separate pine trees. With Evangeline watching them, Rab tied them to their separate trees, Wool first and then Matty Rio.

With the two men bound so tight against their respective tree trunks that they could do nothing more than stand, Rab and Evangeline made a quick breakfast in preparation for a long ride out of the mountains. When their breakfast was done and the fire buried, they saddled their own horses and cinched the saddles on the other horses.

One at a time, Rab put Matty Rio and Wool on the stolen horses they'd saddled. When they were on, Rab used a length of rope to tie their ankles under the horse's bellies.

"You boys try to make a run, and you'll be in a mess if you come out of the saddle," Rab said to them. "You'll get caught up under your horses and trampled. I intend to get you out of here and back to Las Vegas, but if you cause trouble along the way it'll go poorly for you."

At that, Rab and Evangeline mounted the blue roan and the buckskin.

Evangeline took the point, leading the way back along the old Indian path that would take them back to the dry wash that would lead them all the way back to the Rio Grande.

Matty Rio and then Wool rode behind her, and Rab took his place behind Wool.

The other two stolen horses that Matty and Wool had along as spare mounts followed up behind Rab. He did not bother dragging the horses on leads. They would follow.

Cromwell didn't much care for the order of march. He liked to be up front on a trail. But other than a few times when Rab had to draw up to slow him down some, he didn't make much of a fuss about it.

They'd not gone more than a couple of miles when Wool's blanket started to come undone from where he'd tied it behind his saddle. Wadded instead of rolled, it fell loose easily.

Rab started to ride up ahead to deal with it, knowing the flapping blanket would aggravate the mare Wool was riding, but then he realized the blanket had taken an odd shape, stiff at one end where it should have been flopping around.

Rab let Cromwell wander closer to Wool's mare, and as he got up close, he saw that Wool had concealed a six-shooter inside the blanket. Rab figured it must have been with him under the blanket when Rab snuck into their camp and woke them up. Wool came up with his knife, but his six-gun remained hidden. That was the true reason he didn't want to roll his blanket.

They walked along through the forest of pine and fir, and Rab reached into his pocket for his pipe.

He could have taken the gun out from under the blanket without any trouble. It was tied in, but Rab was fairly certain that he could ride up beside Wool and have the gun before Wool could react and try to do anything about it. But for the moment, he decided to leave it where it was, curious to see what Wool would try and when he would try it.

"You keep us at this pace, we'll cross the Rio Grande before dark," Rab called ahead to Evangeline.

Not having to follow tracks meant they could move at a quicker pace. A journey that had taken two days could be done in one now that they knew for sure where they were going.

***

Chavez woke earlier than his counterparts.

He was ahead of them several miles and had camped at the edge of a wide grassland. At the far end of the grass field a large mountain peak covered in pine rose high above the field. In its center was a dome mound.

It was the dome mound that spooked Chavez.

He'd seen it as he set up camp the night before and thought little of it until he'd opened a can of beans and was eating his supper. Then he became curious about the odd dome. It was far out in the grassland, much larger than any building in Las Vegas or Santa Fe – even larger than the churches – and covered in fir trees.

As he ate, Chavez convinced himself the mound must be some sort of Indian burial ground. At the base of the dome were enormous boulders and rock outcroppings, some the size of a house, and Chavez began to wonder if those stones were perhaps adobe buildings of a pueblo. He was too far, and the light too scant, to know for sure. He was only a step away, then, from believing that the place was haunted by the spirits of generations of dead Indians. Through the night, Chavez imagined every gust of wind rattling through the pine branches above must surely be a Hopi or Navajo or Apache spirit come to scalp him. If his horse nickered or stamped at the ground, it was enough to make Chavez weep with fright.

He did not sleep, and when the first gray light of dawn appeared in the sky, Chavez decided to forgo his breakfast, pack his camp, and start back the way he'd come.

Though he wasn't sure where he was, he knew he wasn't in Albuquerque.

He reasoned that whatever had happened with the posse was done now. He thought that surely Matty Rio, Wool, Eduardo, and Caleb were taken prisoner and the posse was gone, for of course he did not know that Caleb Morgan was shot by Wool.

Maybe, Chavez thought, Matty Rio and the others had managed to drive off the posse and had made their escape to Albuquerque.

Doubtful as it was, Chavez thought maybe it was possible.

Either way, he was going the wrong direction. Chavez wasn't much for finding his way in open country, but he knew that he needed to go back and find the river and follow it on its southward flow.

So as soon as he had light enough to pick his way back through the forest, Chavez abandoned the open grassland and left the ghosts of generations behind him and started back down toward the Rio Grande.

- 29 -

The Rio Grande valley was the ideal place to camp, particularly for the horses exhausted from so many days of riding.

The valley offered good grass for forage, and good shade from the tall cottonwoods. They had fresh water from the river, which was important because they wouldn't have good water again until they reached Santa Fe.

Crossing the river at the ford was no problem. Even at its deepest, the water barely splashed against the horses' bellies.

Rab kept a close eye on Wool as they crossed the river. If the man was going to try for his gun, a river crossing was a good place to do it. But Wool never reached for the gun nor gave any indication he was thinking about it.

"We'll camp here tonight," Rab told his prisoners as they reined in their horses. "In the morning we'll leave early, and we won't stop riding until we're in Santa Fe."

Wool and Matty Rio were both tied to their horses. Rab got Wool down first while Evangeline kept a watch on both of them with her Winchester. Once he was off the horse, Rab tied Wool to a cottonwood.

He pressed him against the tree and then looped a rope around Wool's wrists. When it was good and taut, Rab looked around the tree at him with a grin.

"You should have tried for the gun when we crossed the river," Rab said, his voice low so that the others wouldn't hear. "That was the best chance you had. I don't mind telling you that I'm disappointed you didn't make a move for it. I was eager for the chance to kill you. Now you tell me, why'd you shoot Caleb Morgan?"

Bud Woolery shrugged his shoulders as best he could, tied against the tree the way he was.

"I saw him standing out there," Wool said. "He was standing up on a rock. We told him to stay with the horses, and he didn't. So I shot him."

"That's it?" Rab asked.

"I guess. I like to shoot things when I'm angry, and coming down out of that slot canyon I was angry to be running away from you. I saw Caleb and I shot him."

Rab didn't say anything. He just walked to Matty Rio and took him down from his horse. Matty wanted to stretch his legs and complained of being stiff, but Rab wasn't in a generous mood. He pushed the man over to a tree and bound his wrists around it.

As he unsaddled their horses, Rab uncovered the Remington six-shooter under Wool's blanket. He turned the cylinder to empty each chamber and threw the rounds and then the gun into the Rio Grande.

Evangeline swore when she realized Wool had been armed the whole time, but Rab assured her that he'd been aware of the gun and had kept an eye on Wool.

Rab collected firewood and got a campfire going, but in doing the work he was thinking about Caleb Morgan. He still felt a rage over the way Matty Rio and these others had turned Caleb against everything the boy knew to be right and led him toward everything that was wrong.

And as he collected firewood, Rab began to realize that the rage existed, in part, because he was jealous. Ever since Caleb was young, even before he came to live with Rab and Evangeline at the ranch, Caleb had thought Rab Sinclair was something of a hero. And somehow, Matty Rio with his slick talk and his fancy duds, had replaced Rab in Caleb's imagination.

As he came to realize that some part of his rage existed because his feelings were hurt, Rab got all the angrier.

He started thinking about the callous and blithe way that Wool talked about killing his victims. And that's when he remembered the Indian woman, shot dead on the tabletop of the white cliffs back across the river.

The sun was already moving far to the west, but

they had a couple of hours of daylight left. There was almost enough daylight left for what Rab had in mind. The ride back to the slot canyon wasn't more than five miles. It was a mile hike up through the canyon to the mesa top, or thereabouts.

"I'm taking Wool for a ride," Rab announced, standing up over the fire he'd just made.

Wool, tied against the tree, snatched his head around. For the first time he felt a pit of fear in his stomach.

"What do you mean a ride?" Wool asked, a nervous bite to his tone.

Evangeline gave Rab a concerned look, but she didn't argue with him.

"Don't untie Matty Rio for anything," Rab said. "Leave him tied to that tree. Even if a big ol' bear comes into camp and you have to mount up and ride away, you leave him tied there. Don't take any chances with him."

"What are you going to do?" Evangeline asked.

"Mr. Woolery has a bit of unfinished business," Rab said.

They took the spare horses.

Rab tied Wool's ankles under the horse's belly again but this time also took the precaution of tying Wool's wrists to the saddle horn. He pulled the horse along on a lead.

"What are you doing with me?" Wool asked after they'd splashed back across the Rio Grande.

"We have some unfinished business, and we're going to finish it."

Rab went at a lope toward the tall white cliffs

looming tall in front of them, and both horses took the rough terrain well. He rode in silence with Wool behind him, occasionally glancing over his shoulder to be sure that Wool hadn't somehow worked free of his ropes.

When they neared the slot canyon, Rab reined in and dropped from his saddle. He untied Wool's ropes and when the man was down from his horse, Rab looped the rope around Wool's wrists and knotted it with his hands in front of him so that Wool would still be able to climb to the top of the mesa.

They moved quickly through the slot canyon, Rab pushing Wool as they went, and always staying within arm's reach of him so that if he tried anything, Rab would be able to easily knock him down.

The sun was sinking low in the west when they topped the rim of the mesa, and Rab knew they would cross back over the Rio Grande in the dark.

He pushed Wool along toward the center of the mesa.

"What are you going to do to me?" Wool asked.

Rab did not answer him but continued to push him forward until they neared the slight figure lying prone on the ground. Already the birds had been at the body, though it did not appear that any animals had been.

"Bury her," Rab said. "Rocks will do, though I should make you tote her below and find a decent place to dig a grave."

Bud Woolery turned around to face Rab Sinclair. The skin around Wool's eyes was still red from the coffee Rab had thrown in his face. Wool's eyes were bloodshot. He was sweating from the strain of the hike up through the slot canyon and the climbing they had to do on the slope.

"Are you a lunatic?" Bud Woolery demanded. "You brought me all the way back here to bury a squaw."

"You killed her," Rab said lightly. "You bury her. Too many other folks – me included – have had to bury your dead. This one is your responsibility."

"Well, untie my wrists," Wool said, holding his hands out in front of him.

Rab shook his head.

"I don't think so," he said. "You can pick up a rock with your hands bound. Now get to it. And if I don't think you're going to be done before the sun drops below the horizon, I'll throw you off this cliff and finish the job myself."

Wool went to work, and it amused Rab to see Wool's frequent glances to the west to mark the location of the sun.

As Wool piled rocks on top of the dead Indian woman, Rab stood by and watched his progress. He smoked his pipe, filling it several times with tobacco and burning it out. It was the first long smoke he'd had all day.

The evening breeze blowing over the mesa was warm, a hint of the coming summer.

"Pack those rocks tight," Rab said. "You're burying a body. You took away everything this woman was on this earth. All the love she had for family, all the joy she ever felt, all the memories she made. You stole all that from the earth when you killed her. And you stole from her everything good that was ever going to happen to her. Time with her children, if she had any. Time with a man she loved, if there was one. You took away every sunset she might have enjoyed, every breeze that she might have felt. And I reckon you did your part to make certain her final hours in this world were misery and torment and violation."

Wool heard the words, but if they resonated or caused even a hint of guilt, Rab couldn't see it on the boy's face. Bud Woolery was just mean.

"You took her from this earth, so now you bury her to return her to it. You understand?"

"She's just an Injun squaw," Bud Woolery said.

Rab considered giving the boy a smash in the head with the heavy barrel of the Dragoon, but instead he let it go.

"And you're just a no-good outlaw who murders unarmed women, but when they're done stretching your neck, they'll dig a hole for you," Rab said.

Wool narrowed his eyes and stared hard at Rab Sinclair.

"Ain't no hangman's noose gonna choke me," he said. "Cause there ain't no jail that's gonna hold me."

As Rab drew on his pipe, a mocking grin crossed his face. He blew smoke out into the wind and then said: "You'd better pray to God in Heaven that the jail does hold you, because if you ever get loose, I'm coming for you. And I promise I won't be saving you for a judge or a jury."

***

The last remnants of dusk were disappearing as they neared the Rio Grande.

"I ain't going take a chance with you crossing that river in the dark," Rab said.

He reined in and dropped down from his horse and got Wool down also. He tied Wool's wrists behind his back and then looped a rope around Wool's arms, securing them fast against his sides.

"We'll walk across the river," Rab said. "The horses can trail behind us."

"If I slip, I'll drown," Wool said.

"If you slip, I'll lift you up," Rab said.

"What if I go under and you can't find me?" Wool said.

"Then you'll drown," Rab conceded without much concern.

As it was, they made the walk across without any trouble. Rab loosened his gunbelt and put it around his saddle horn and took off his boots and socks, pushing one each into his saddlebags. He stripped out of his trousers to keep those from getting soaked. He did Wool the courtesy of removing his boots as well. If a man's boots filled with water, he'd wear blisters pretty bad the next day. And he also helped the bound man out of his pants.

They trod through the water that came up to their thighs at the deepest parts. Rab kept his knife on his belt as they crossed the river, but he never had to make a grab for it. He did not know if Wool was finally cowed or was just waiting for a better moment to try to get away.

On the opposite bank, Rab dried himself with an old towel in his saddlebags and put his pants back on. He then dried his feet and slid them back into his boots, leaving his socks in the saddlebags because he'd done a rush job of it and his feet weren't thoroughly dry yet. Though he'd done Wool the courtesy of removing his trousers and boots, Rab did not now give them back. A few bruises on the soles of his feet wouldn't hurt him too bad.

Ahead they could see a fire burning where Rab and Evangeline had made camp. The fire was up a good bit higher than Rab would have liked. Though they were far enough from the mountain hunting grounds of the Navajo, it was never wise to announce your presence with too large a fire. Only a man who was scared of the dark would build such a large fire just for camping.

Rab reached out and took hold of the rope binding Bud Woolery.

"What happened to your friend Chavez?" Rab asked in a whisper.

"We told you," Wool said. "He run off."

Rab held the ropes fast so that Wool didn't move any closer to the camp. The horses were behind him. His Winchester rifle was in its scabbard on his saddle, his Colt Dragoon was in its holster, still hanging from the saddle horn.

Something was wrong up ahead. Rab didn't like the size of that fire one bit.

"That boy Chavez, is he a bit skittish?" Rab asked, still whispering.

"What do you mean by skittish?" Wool asked.

"Is he afraid of the dark?"

Wool shrugged, as much as he could with his arms bound to his sides.

Rab had turned his lariat around Wool four or five times, pulling the rope taut. He'd stuck the excess down one loop at Wool's back. Now he pulled out that excess, tied the loose end into a slipknot, and then he stuck a leg behind Wool's calves and knocked the man flat on his back.

Wool let out a loud exclamation and then began to complain about the treatment, but Rab ignored him.

He did it rough on purpose. Rab worked the loop around Wool's ankles and then jerked the knot tight so hard that Wool was flipped around to his stomach.

"You shut your mouth and don't move," Rab said. "If something's wrong up ahead, I'm coming back here and shooting you just so I don't have to worry about watching my back."

Rab wasn't sure if it was an idle threat or not.

Suddenly he had a pit in his stomach, worried for Evangeline and regretting forcing Wool up to the top of that mesa to bury the Indian woman.

The campfire, built too high, cast flickering shadows around the campsite. Rab did not think he had any choice but to just walk into the campsite and see what happened. He left Wool hogtied on the ground and led the horses toward the camp. He took his time going forward, trying to see anything within the camp that might provide a clue as to what was going on.

All Rab knew for sure was that the campfire was built too large.

But he did not see Evangeline near the fire. When he checked the tree where he'd tied Matty Rio, the man was gone.

A horse nickered not far from where Rab was approaching. It was Cromwell, and Rab thought it sounded like a warning.

In the light from the fire he could see the blue roan and the buckskin. He could see the two horses that Matty

Rio and Wool had ridden all that day.

But there was another horse. Rab recognized it as one of his own, a large draft horse that had been among those stolen from his ranch. It was the horse he'd been tracking along with the horses Matty Rio and Wool had with them.

There was no question that Chavez had ridden into the camp.

The horse he was leading nuzzled against Rab's back, giving him a light push and reminding him that his Colt was hung around the saddle horn.

"Throw up your hands."

The sound came from the shadows to Rab's right under some cottonwood trees. It was Matty Rio.

"I've got your woman's rifle," Matty said. "Put your hands up or I'll shoot you."

Rab stood his ground. He needed to buy a little time to see how this would play out. He wouldn't be able to get to his guns, not without being shot. But Rab Sinclair knew that there were always more weapons at hand than the obvious ones, it was just an issue of finding them.

"Where's Wool?" Matty Rio asked. "What did you do to him?"

Rab didn't move. He didn't put up his hands or go for his gun. He held his position, pulling the lead rope a little away from him to keep the horse from nuzzling again.

"You're going to make this worse on yourself," Rab said. "Where's Evangeline?"

"I'm here," Evangeline said, speaking from the shadows where Matty Rio's voice was coming from.

Rab squinted at the cottonwoods, but he couldn't see anyone clearly.

"Chavez ride into camp?" Rab asked.

"I'm sorry," Evangeline said. I heard him crossing the river and just thought it was you coming back. He's got a shotgun on me."

"Shut up, both of you!" Matty Rio whined. "Put your hands up!"

Rab still didn't put his hands up. He just held the horse and stood his ground.

Even if he had a gun in his hand, he couldn't see into the cottonwoods to know where to shoot. He might just as easily hit Evangeline, or nothing. Though like as not he'd hit a tree or fat Chavez – the bigger targets. He needed to draw Matty Rio and Chavez into the open.

"Turn the woman loose," Rab said.

Sinclair purposefully kept his eyes off the fire. He needed his eyes to adjust to the dark to give him a chance. As he kept his eyes away from the fire, he took a couple of steps toward the fire. Now Matty Rio and Chavez were watching him with the fire right beside him, a fire that was putting off too much light and – whether they realized it or not – a fire that was about to leave them blind. In a moment, Rab knew, Matty Rio and Chavez would need to be able to see in the dark, but because they were now looking into the fire, they would have a harder time seeing in the dark.

Rab pulled the lead so that the horse stepped a little closer to him. When he did, Rab whipped the slack on the lead to slap the horse's hind quarter. The horse let out a loud squeal and darted forward, agitating all the horses so that in a moment there was pawing at the ground and stamping of hooves and general commotion.

The moment he smacked the horse with the lead, Rab also darted forward, running in front of the fire and then into the shadows of the cottonwoods. He did it with his eyes all but shut to block out as much of the light as possible. A rifle cracked and he heard a bullet smash timber nearby, but in an instant Matty Rio and Chavez had lost sight of him.

Rab crouched low.

"Dammit!" Matty Rio shouted. "You show yourself of Chavez will cut this woman in two!"

In the dark shadows under the cottonwoods, Rab moved toward their voices even though he could not yet see them. He knew they couldn't be more than fifteen feet in front of him. He felt his way, finding the rough, deeply lined bark of the cottonwoods.

His feet struck a branch, but he stopped moving before he got tied up in it and tripped.

"Show yourself!" Matty Rio shouted again.

Rab's hand curled around the antler handle of the big Bowie knife he wore on his belt. He slid it from its leather scabbard and twisted his hand so that the long blade was flat against his own forearm, hiding it so that the metal did not catch the reflection of the fire and give him away.

He stepped forward around a big cottonwood.

"Where is he?" Matty Rio hissed.

"I didn't see where he went," Chavez said.

Their voices led Rab in the right direction. And then, in the faint light from the fire, Sinclair saw the amber sweat beading on the fat man's forehead.

Rab held his breath, peering into the blackness in front of him. His eyes were starting to adjust. He could see the fire reflecting in Evangeline's eyes. Chavez stood behind her, maybe two feet. Just enough to have the barrel of the shotgun into her back.

Rab reached out into the darkness with his foot and worked his foot under the branch that had nearly tripped him. His leg was extended as far as it would go, but he didn't need much leverage. With just a flick of his ankle, he kicked the branch into the air.

It made a tremendous racket, and being so close to them it was sure to startle them terribly. Both Matty Rio and Chavez reacted.

Matty Rio fired the Winchester at the noise. It was a wild shot, and Rab worried for his horses that were down range.

Chavez, one big hand wrapped around Evangeline's arm, dragged her away and pulled the trigger of the shotgun. Pellets cut through leaves and branches, and the heavy echo of the explosion banged inside all their heads. The big gun was more than even Chavez could handle with one hand, and it snapped back on the recoil and dragged Chavez's hand with it.

Rab had seen the gun already and knew that it was a single-shot. Chavez, while he'd be hell in a fist fight just because of his size, was now not much of a threat.

Matty Rio worked the lever on the Winchester, but Rab was too near to him. Before he had the new round chambered, Rab Sinclair launched himself from his spot behind the cottonwood, the heavy Bowie knife, catching the light from the fire, glowing orange in the dark space between them.

The first cut of the knife sliced across Matty Rio's chest from shoulder to shoulder. The cut was not deep enough to be mortal, but it sent a searing, electric pain straight into the man's head.

He dropped the Winchester and fell away, clutching at his chest.

Evangeline squirmed to break free from Chavez's grip, and she let out a little shout.

Chavez was of two minds.

He knew that he couldn't let Evangeline go because she was their best bargaining chip for subduing Rab Sinclair. But he also knew that he needed to reload his shotgun, a feat he could not accomplish with one hand.

So in lieu of deciding which task to achieve, Chavez managed to do neither. He held to Evangeline's arm too long to get the shotgun reloaded, and when he finally decided he needed to shoot Rab Sinclair, he turned loose of Evangeline.

Evangeline went to the ground without a second thought. She'd seen Matty Rio drop the rifle, and the yellow receiver that gave the Winchester its "Yellow Boy" nickname shined like gold in the light of the fire. As soon as Chavez let loose of her, Evangeline dove, and she came to her knees with the Winchester's forestock in her left hand and working the lever with her right.

When Chavez released his grip on Evangeline, Rab struck the large, open target with his knife.

He drove the knife into the fat man's throat, and then sliced it away.

Chavez collapsed to the ground, choking on his own blood.

Evangeline did not give Matty Rio an opportunity to surrender.

With the rifle's barrel so close that it almost touched his chest, Evangeline fired a shot. She dropped the lever and let loose a second shot, just to be safe.

- 30 -

"Someone's coming," Evangeline said.

They were sitting together in the shade on the front porch of their cabin. Spring had turned to summer early. In the month since they'd returned home, the white patches on Hermits Peak had all disappeared and the sun seemed intent on cooking everything it touched.

Rab had a small pocketknife that he was using to scrape tar and resin from the bowl of his pipe, and he wasn't paying any attention to the valley out in front of them. He looked up and saw three men riding along the trail that led through the valley and up to the cabin and its outbuildings. They had just dropped down off the main trail above, and at this distance, he did not recognize the riders. He put his eyes on the rifle leaning against the porch railing, though he knew it was there without looking.

He went back to work on his pipe.

Evangeline leaned forward from her chair, squinting at the men in the distance.

"Is one of them Vazquez?" she asked.

Rab knocked the pipe against the porch railing and then blew through the stem to clear it. He set the pocketknife down and reached for his tobacco pouch before looking up.

"I believe it is," he said.

"Is today Friday?" Evangeline asked.

Sometimes on the ranch it was easy to lose track of what day of the week it was. That was one of the things Rab liked about living on the ranch.

"Now that you mention it, I believe it is," Rab said.

Evangeline cut her eyes sideways at him and grinned. Rab watched her. She had a strong chin. He liked that about her.

"Look at that," Evangeline said, a note of surprise in her voice. "One of them is a soldier."

Rab could see now the cavalryman's uniform – the dark blue pants with the yellow stripe and the light blue shirt, the tan hat.

"Sure enough," Rab said. "I hope you're not in trouble with the federal government."

Evangeline shook her head and rolled her eyes at him.

As they came nearer, Rab recognized Lieutenant Eddie Matthews from the Fort Union quartermaster's office.

He dug his pipe into the tobacco pouch and filled the bowl, then struck a match and lit it.

"Howdy Rab!" Vazquez called as the three mounted men rode up toward the house. "Hope you don't mind a visit."

"A deputy sheriff and an army lieutenant," Rab said. "That's a passel of government riding out across my valley."

Vazquez nodded as he swung a leg over his horse and stepped down from the saddle. He hitched his horse to a post in the yard out front.

"I ran into Lt. Matthews and his brother in town. They were looking for you, and I was on my way out here anyway so I offered to show them the way."

Rab glanced at Matthews and the other man.

"Y'all have a seat," Rab said, though the only two chairs on the front porch were already occupied.

Vazquez walked around the front railing and leaned against it, and Matthews and the other man both did as well.

"I come to tell you it's finished with Bud Woolery and Eduardo," Vazquez said. "Hangman got them yesterday at dawn."

Rab nodded and glanced at Evangeline to see how she took the news. Her face, with her pretty eyes and the strong chin, remained impassive.

"To tell the truth, I didn't think that boy Wool was going to make his appointment with the hangman," Rab said. "I figured of all of them, he'd be the first one I'd have to kill."

Vazquez nodded.

"He swore just about every day since the trial he was going to bust out and come after you," Vazquez said. "That boy was rotten all the way to the ground."

Vazquez started to say something else and then stopped himself. He glanced at Lt. Matthews.

"Anyway," Vazquez said. "I think these men were looking to have a word with you. Mind if I walk my horse down to the barn and fetch him some hay?"

Rab nodded at Vazquez and then turned his attention to the army quartermaster's clerk.

"Lt. Matthews, what brings you down this way?" Rab asked.

"Last time you was up at Fort Union, we talked about you maybe selling this place to my brother," Lt. Matthews said. "Well, this is my brother Davis Matthews, just come from back east. And we thought we'd ride down here and see if you had given any thought to it."

"To selling the place?" Rab asked.

"That's right," Lt. Matthews said. "We'd offer a fair price for the land, the buildings, and your livestock."

From where he sat, Rab could look across the valley to a notch at the southeastern end and see the peak of Starvation Mountain. He could glance east and just see the top of Hermit's Peak overlooking Las Vegas.

He could not now see the mustangs that once roamed his property, not that they'd have been out in this heat anyway. But just a few weeks ago, Rab could have counted on them. When it cooled off closer to sunset, they'd have made a run up out of the juniper and gone to the grassland near one of the creeks.

But not now.

After Matty Rio – or probably Wool – shot a few of them, the herd abandoned the valley. Those wild horses that had shared this ranch with Rab and Evangeline were now gone, the same as Caleb Morgan was now gone.

"I ain't much for ranching," Rab said. "But there's a whole lot about this spot that appeals to me. I don't know that I'd care to sell it. On the other hand, we've talked about settling higher up in the hills. There's a valley or two up there we've noted."

He looked at Evangeline to see if she had a thought.

"I don't know what we'd do if we didn't have cattle," Evangeline said, not looking at Lt. Matthews. "Settling higher up has an appeal, but we've still got to earn a living, wherever we are."

Rab took a draw on his pipe and blew the smoke out slowly. He kept his eyes on Evangeline. He could see by the expression on her face that she was thinking.

"Of course," she said. "One thing that speaks in favor of it. It's sorrowful to me to sit here and see Caleb Morgan's cabin sitting empty. It's a daily reminder of a thing I'd just as soon forget."

Rab nodded, thinking of the mustangs.

"It is that."

They talked for a while with Eddie Matthews and his brother Davis. They spoke of the size of the herd and its value. Rab pointed out to them the landmarks they could see that showed boundaries of the ranch. A high hill that way. A tall ponderosa a little ways farther. He spoke with some pride about the creeks that ran through the ranch.

"Flowing water year-round," he noted. "Not many places around here can say that. We've had a couple of the creeks dry up for a month or three, but never had all of them go dry at once."

Rab got up and got both men a drink. They talked a while longer. Davis talked about some of the news from back east, complaining that women from Illinois to Maryland were crusading against liquor and setting up temperance unions. He spoke of traveling west. He'd come by train all the way to Denver and then took a stagecoach south. He swore the stage ride from Denver to Las Vegas was enough to convince him that he'd never return east if he had to do it in a stagecoach.

"I reckon it won't be long before they've laid rails through here," Davis said shrewdly. He'd already marked Rab Sinclair as a man who wouldn't want to live anywhere near a railroad depot.

In the end, Lt. Matthews and his brother offered a price for the ranch. Rab, who was no hand at real estate transactions, didn't know if it was a fair price or not, but he knew it was a high price. Even so, they reached no immediate conclusion on the ranch.

"We'll be staying in the hotel on the plaza for another three days," Eddie Matthews said. "After that, I reckon we'll head back to the fort. Think about our offer, Rab. If it suits you, come and find us."

The two men did not wait for Vazquez to come back up from the barn. They seemed to sense he had more to say in private, and they rode off together to leave Vazquez to make his way back to town on his own.

After they'd ridden out of sight, Vazquez came up from the barn, leading his horse.

"I did have one other thing I wanted to mention to you," he said.

"The other bit of news I have is that Caleb came in on this morning's stagecoach from Santa Fe," Vazquez said. "He's in the jail up in Las Vegas right now."

After Caleb Morgan was shot, Vazquez managed to get him back to a doctor in Santa Fe. The doctor swore it was unlikely he'd make it another day, but he did what he could for Caleb before taking him to St. Vincent's hospital where the nuns cared for him. What probably saved Caleb's life more than anything was that two of the nuns who started the hospital back in '65 had been nurses in the War Between the States. They were better suited to dealing with bullet wounds, even bad bullet wounds, than the doctor.

When Rab and Evangeline returned to Las Vegas to put Bud Woolery in the jail with Eduardo, Vazquez told them where they could find Caleb.

They spent one night at the ranch and then rode to Santa Fe. Rab carried with him a fifty dollar donation for the nuns and another fifty dollars that he gave to Caleb.

"That's the last you'll get from me," he told the boy. "What you do from now on is up to you, but you'll not do it on my ranch. Don't come back there. You stole from me and you partnered up with thieves and killers, and you won't be welcomed back."

They were hard words to say, and hard words to hear. But Rab's mind was made up, and Caleb already knew he couldn't return to the ranch.

"The warrant for Caleb," Vazquez said, taking a

folded piece of paper out of his pocket. "Horse theft is all that's on here. His part in the rest of it was mild enough that Romero isn't going to pursue it. But the horses were stolen from you, and so it's your prerogative to take him to trial if you want."

Rab looked at the piece of paper in Vazquez's hand and then turned his eyes to Evangeline. She gave a small shake of her head. Rab knew where she stood. She'd not argued against the banishment, but she did not want to see Caleb imprisoned or hanged.

"What if I don't want to press the charge?" Rab asked.

Vazquez shrugged.

"Put a match to this warrant, and when I get back I'll open up the jail door and set Caleb loose," Vazquez said.

"Is that justice?" Rab said. "Does Caleb get what he deserves?"

"It's mercy," Evangeline said. "Did Christ on the cross not forgive a thief?"

"He did," Rab acknowledged.

"Then maybe we should do no less. Burn the warrant, Rabbie," Evangeline said. "He's punished enough and learned his lesson."

Rab looked to Vazquez and raised his eyebrows, inviting the deputy sheriff to have a say.

"They was your horses, Rab," Vazquez said. "I reckon that makes this your decision."

Rab nodded his head toward Evangeline.

"They were her horses as much as they were mine," Rabbie said. "And I reckon we managed to get them all back."

He struck a match and held it to a corner of the paper. Vazquez held it so that the fire would climb the paper, and when it neared his fingers he tossed the paper down onto the dirt.

"That's settled," Vazquez said. "My custom with horse thieves is to see them hang. But I reckon this time around I'll be satisfied to watch this one walk away."

"What will happen to Caleb?" Evangeline asked.

Vazquez shrugged. He glanced at Rab, whose face was impassive.

"Folks think well of Caleb," Vazquez said. "His involvement in all of this isn't widely known. Someone will hire him."

Rab handed Vazquez a couple of silver coins.

"Put him up in the Plaza Hotel," Rab said. "Tell him to find Lt. Matthews. There's probably work up at Fort Union. And if there's not, maybe the lieutenant's brother will be looking to hire someone who can work cattle in the next few days."

Vazquez took the coins.

"They told me they was thinking of making an offer on your place," Vazquez said. "You planning to sell?"

"I don't know yet," Rab said. "But even if I don't, the lieutenant's brother will be getting into something out here. Whatever it is, he could do worse than hiring Caleb. I don't expect that boy will ever cause trouble again, and he's a good hand."

Rab filled his pipe and lit it as he and Evangeline watched Vazquez ride away.

"We've talked of moving on from here," Rab said.

"We have," Evangeline said. "And it's not been the same with Caleb gone."

"And the mustangs," Rab said. "I took a lot of pleasure in watching those horses."

Evangeline looked far off through the valley.

"It was hard for Caleb," she said. "He never wanted any of this to happen, but I think once he got caught up with Matty Rio and that group he didn't know how to get out of it."

Rab nodded.

"I wish he'd listened to me," Rab said. "I tried to warn him."

Evangeline nodded sadly.

"It's hard when you're young and all you hear is people preaching at you," she said. "I suppose sometimes young folks just have to learn their lessons for themselves."

Later in the afternoon, Rab and Evangeline went to the pasture and caught the blue roan and the buckskin. They saddled the horses and rode out across the valley ranch, checking on the cattle and keeping their eyes open for signs of predators that might harass the herd. They stopped and spoke to Kuwatee, letting him know about the offer on the ranch. Then they rode a little ways up a hill where they had a good view of Hermit's Peak standing tall over Las Vegas. North of there were a number of pastoral grassland valleys nestled in the hills.

Rab leaned forward and rubbed Cromwell's neck with his open palm.

"Maybe we should start over somewhere else," he

said. "Maybe we've had our share of this place, and maybe someone else should have it now."

"Maybe we should," Evangeline agreed. "Lt. Matthews' brother seemed like a decent man. I expect he'd do well here."

"He'll do well wherever he sets up," Rab said. "His brother is making the buying decisions for the Fort Union quartermaster. I reckon if we don't sell the ranch we can expect to lose our contract, anyway."

"That speaks in favor of selling," Evangeline said with a wry grin.

Then she said, "That was kind what you did for Caleb."

"You're the one who said to burn the warrant."

"I mean the money for the hotel, and sending him to Lt. Matthews' brother," Evangeline said.

"All your talk of the thief on the cross with Christ," Rab said. "It reminded me of what my father used to preach about God's mercy and God's grace. Mercy, he said, is God withholding from us the judgment we deserve. But grace is giving to us a kindness we don't deserve."

Evangeline smiled brightly at him, and it made Rab happy to see her full of joy again. Since they'd come back to the ranch, there were times when Evangeline seemed wistful, and Rab knew the cause was her worry over Caleb.

"Rabbie Sinclair," she said, grinning at him.

"What?" he asked.

"Your kindness to Caleb isn't putting him up in a hotel for a couple of days. Grace is selling the ranch to Davis Matthews."

Rab pulled a rein to one side and gave the blue roan some leg to get him started back on a walk.

"Mercy and grace, those ain't my stock and trade," Rab said. "I'm just thinking maybe it's time for you and me to make tracks."

The buckskin didn't need any encouragement and started on its own following behind Cromwell.

"All right," Evangeline said. "Where do you want to make tracks to?"

"I reckon we'll figure that out when we get there," Rab said in his easy way, laying the reins on the blue roan's neck to cut him back toward the west.

the end

ABOUT THE AUTHOR

Robert Peecher is the author of more than a score of Western novels. He is former journalist who spent 20 years working as a reporter and editor for daily and weekly newspapers in Georgia.

Together with his wife Jean, he's raised three fine boys and a mess of dogs. An avid outdoorsman who enjoys hiking trails and paddling rivers, Peecher's novels are inspired by a combination of his outdoor adventures, his fascination with American history, and his love of the one truly American genre of novel: The Western.

For more information and to keep up with his latest releases, we would encourage you to visit his website (mooncalfpress.com) and sign up for his twice-monthly e-newsletter.

OTHER NOVELS BY ROBERT PEECHER

THE LODERO WESTERNS: Two six-shooters and a black stallion. When Lodero makes a graveside vow to track down the mystery of his father's disappearance, it sends Lodero and Juan Carlos Baca on an epic quest through the American Southwest. Don't miss this great 4-book series!

THE TWO RIVERS STATION WESTERNS: Jack Bell refused to take the oath from the Yankees at Bennett Place. Instead, he stole a Union cavalry horse and started west toward a new life in Texas. There he built a town and raised a family, but he'll have to protect his way of life behind a Henry rifle and a Yankee Badge.

ANIMAS FORKS: Animas Forks, Colorado, is the largest city in west of the Mississippi (at 14,000 feet). The town has everything you could want in a Frontier Boomtown: cutthroats, ne'er-do-wells, whores, backshooters, drunks, thieves, and murderers. Come on home to Animas Forks in this fun, character-driven series.

TRULOCK'S POSSE: When the Garver gang guns down the town marshal, Deputy Jase Trulock must form a posse to chase down the Garvers before they reach the outlaw town of Profanity.

FIND THESE AND OTHER NOVELS BY
ROBERT PEECHER AT AMAZON.COM

Made in the USA
Coppell, TX
17 September 2020

38223180R00173